The Story
of a Teenager
with Bulimia

❖❖❖❖❖❖❖❖❖❖❖❖❖

Liza F. Hall

gürze books

PERK!
The Story of a Teenager with Bulimia

©1997 by Liza F. Hall

Cover design: Abacus Graphics, Oceanside, CA
Cover illustration: Kitty Meek, Fallbrook, CA

Published by:
Gürze Books
PO Box 2238
Carlsbad CA 92018
(760)434-7533

Library of Congress Cataloging-in-Publication Data

Hall, Liza F., 1961-
  Perk! : the story of a teenager with bulimia / Liza F. Hall.
        p. cm.
  Summary: Unhappy about boys, her parents, and her body, Perk, a
high school student, becomes a victim of bulimia and resorts to binge
eating and forced vomiting to gain control of her life.
  ISBN 0-936077-27-1 (alk. paper)
  1. Bulimia—fiction. [1. Self-esteem—Fiction.] I. Title.
PZ7.H14575Pe   1997
[Fic]—dc21   97-8718
                                                       CIP
                                                        AC

Acknowledgments
❖❖❖❖❖❖❖❖❖❖❖❖❖❖❖❖❖❖❖

I am indebted to the women in my writing group, Helen Galvin, Brooke Romano, Janie Emaus, and Karen Ewen, for their expertise and insights.

Many thanks to the juniors and seniors at Taft High School, Woodland Hills, CA who sat through my lectures on my own personal experience with bulimia and provided me with a wealth of inspiration and information.

I'd also like to thank my husband, Edd; my children, Gilda and Sam Henry; my parents, Jon and Jeanne Forster; and my sister, Lauren Motta, for their encouragement and support.

Finally, thanks to Dr. Ellen Schor Haimoff in New York City for giving the project her blessing, and to Judy Dellar, M.A. in Encino, CA for her expert consultation on *PERK!*

Chapter 1

❖❖❖❖❖❖❖❖❖

I ran my fingers through my hair. Usually it was one of my best features. Today it was stringy and flat. I got my bathrobe from the closet. It seemed twice as heavy as usual. My ribs felt like I had been in a car accident instead of recuperating from three weeks of bronchitis.

I was dying to take a shower. I took a deep breath, which made me cough again. I looked at myself in the mirror as the bathroom filled with steam. I did look really thin. I lost about 15 pounds from being sick. Cool, I thought to myself. It made all the hacking more than worthwhile.

The hot water left me feeling completely spaced out. I had to sit on the toilet while I got dried off to keep from falling over. I caught myself just as I was about to use roll-on deodorant on my face instead of pimple cream.

"Priscilla Sinclair! If you're going to school today, let's get going! I've got a meeting this morning." Mom's voice from the kitchen downstairs made me jump. So did hearing her call me "Priscilla." It meant she was irritated.

"I'm hurrying!" I hollered and gave a couple of good deep coughs to remind her I was sick.

Priscilla was my full name. I was named after an aunt that I had never met. I hated it. Perk is my name, Perk Sinclair.

"Larry, get up! You are such a lazy doggy bone head." I kissed my big black lab on the nose. He groaned and stretched, opening one big brown eye to investigate. I rolled him over and found my favorite shoes. They were squashed and warm.

I lifted my little mouse out of his cage and kissed him on his nose. "Hi, Moonpie. Time to rise and shine, Clementine!" I had rescued Moonpie from a drain-pipe last fall. Sometimes I could get him to stay in my sweatshirt pocket, and he would come to school with me. These were my true best friends, Larry and Moonpie. They knew everything about me.

I gazed at the walls in my room as I pulled on my overalls and turtleneck. They were covered with my artwork; oil paintings, sketches, and collages. I was proud of my room. Last time Dad was up here, he complained about the tacks I was using to attach things to the wall.

"Priscilla, right now. I mean it!" Mom sounded impatient.

I went downstairs slowly. My 14-month-old sister, Bridey, greeted me with a happy shriek from her highchair.

"Hi, Honey Bunny!" I gave her a smoochy kiss on her head. She laughed. She had a great laugh.

"Yo, babe," said Marilyn. Marilyn was Bridey's nanny. She high-fived me. Marilyn was very cool.

"Yo, babe," I replied weakly and smiled. We greeted each other this way every morning.

I wasn't dying to go back to school, but today was the art festival and I was going to be in it. Otherwise, I'd just as soon never go back. Tenth grade was the pits.

I did want to see my best friend, Evvie. Most of all, I wanted to see Dominick. I couldn't help it, I loved him and I always would, no matter what. I knew someday he would see what a good person I was and fall in love with me, too. Until then, I would wait.

"I hope you aren't hungry, Perk. We don't have time for breakfast." Mom lifted Bridey out of her highchair and brushed a stray curl off her forehead with the back of her hand.

Mom was gorgeous. Whenever I thought about her, my chest ached. People were always saying how classy looking she was. She could eat whatever she wanted and never gain any weight. I didn't seem to inherit her genes. It made me crazy.

One time I had overheard my Grandma saying that Mom should never have left such a promising career as a child psychologist in New York City, and especially not to marry someone like my dad. Now my mother was a guidance counselor in my high school, and I got the distinct feeling she wished she had stayed in New York.

"I never eat breakfast anyway, Mom." Sometimes she didn't know anything about me. I grabbed my winter jacket and stuffed a pile of books and papers into my backpack.

Mom kept looking at me as we pulled out onto Route 28. "Jeez, Honey. I notice you've lost some weight. You look good."

I was glad she noticed. I knew she'd be happy about it. "I didn't look fat before, did I?"

"Well of course not, but you do have a tendency to be a little chubby."

I stared at Mom. "So all of those times I asked you if I looked fat and you said no, you were just lying to me."

Mom pulled into the construction site where Dad worked. "Oh, Perk, this weight-thing is always such a big deal for you. If you need to lose a few pounds, so what! Don't worry about it. I need to stop and drop Dad's lunch off."

"I don't want to be late, Mom. It's my first day back." I wanted to get out of the car. If Mom thought I was fat, other people probably did too. I hated to think about that. No wonder Dom didn't pay attention to me.

"You know, that is a completely unattractive expression you have on your face. I wasn't trying to

hurt your feelings. I was trying to be honest with you."
Mom said.

I squinted against the glare of the winter sun hitting the new snow. I screwed up my face hard, to make the crying feeling go away. I saw a figure silhouetted, walking towards the car. It was Dad.

Evvie and I always said that Dad acted like he was in some macho movie with cameras running all the time. He looked like he should be doing commercials in Montana, riding horses and roping cattle. Evvie always got dreamy-eyed around Dad. I suspected she was secretly in love with him. I had quit being surprised when friends would get major crushes on him.

"So the walking wounded is up and about." Dad stuck his head in the car window but looked past me at Mom. He took off thick gloves and blew warm air into his cupped hands. His cheeks were bright red and the sun shone through his silvery gray hair. He smelled cold and clean.

It made me feel weird when he was so close. I wanted to throw my arms around his neck and hold him tight, but I also wanted to get away. The feeling reminded me of when you stuck two magnets together at the wrong end and they pushed at each other. He had a bad temper, and sometimes he scared me.

Mom took the car out of gear and smiled at Dad. "I thought I'd bring you lunch. You're always off at work by the time I get up."

"Thanks, Baby." Dad nodded. He reached across me for the paper bag and thermos. Their fingers touched. Creases appeared at the edges of his eyes which was his version of a smile.

The Volvo pulled back out onto Route 28. I turned the heat up in the car, and opened the vents all the way. Mom made a choking face and opened her window. Looking to the left, the icy Esopus Creek twinkled through the trees. Everything looked fresh and new, which usually made me want to play music really loud, or paint, or rearrange my room. Usually, I loved this time of year. Right now I didn't care that much. I guess it was because I was sick.

I grew up here in Phoenicia, in the Catskill mountains. We had always lived in the same house. My grandpa built it on a little hill overlooking the Esopus. My plan was to graduate high school, and move to New York City as fast as I could. But I knew in my heart I would never love any place as much as that house, and the creek.

I was feeling sick again. When I closed my eyes, they felt burny and it was hard to open them. Little red sparks danced and swirled behind my eyelids. I imagined the fever in my body. I could feel it, all hot, as I breathed. I dozed off and jumped when I heard my mother's voice.

"Perk, are you awake? We're here, Honey."

I rubbed my eyes. My high school always seemed so out of place with the surrounding mountains. It reminded me of a factory.

"Thanks, Mom." I took a quick peek at myself in the car mirror. I looked like I had been sick for a while, but I was thin! I jumped out of the car and flipped my hair forward and back to get it just right.

My legs were wobbly as I ran up the stairway to the front entrance. The first bell had rung and everyone was rushing to get to homeroom.

"Here we go again," I thought. I saw Dom walking down the hall towards me and my heart stopped. He was so gorgeous!

"Hi, Dom!" My voice sounded all little and weird. He walked right by me. My face started burning. I wished I were back in bed. I thought about finding Mom and telling her I was too sick to stay in school today. Instead I turned and hurried to homeroom. I hoped nobody had seen Dom blow me off.

My best friend, Evvie, found me after the bell. "Hey, skinny! It's about time you got your butt out of bed." She grabbed my elbow and swirled me around.

"Hey! Do you really think I look skinny?" It was totally cool to hear her say that.

"Absolutely, positively! Listen, I got the big warning from the Dean of Mean. I can't be late to classes anymore or I'm suspended, so I'll catch ya' during lunch." Evvie blew me a kiss and rushed off to class.

If I could wish to look like anyone, it would be her. Her father was black and her mother was white. Evvie had cream and coffee colored skin. She had lived in New York City almost all of her life, and had taken ballet. Evvie was the most beautiful girl I had ever seen.

At lunch, we ordered buttered hard rolls and tossed a few bags of Doritos and containers of chocolate milk on a tray. I didn't like to eat all this junk food, but Evvie kept loading up the tray. We hurried to find a free table.

Evvie scraped the extra butter off her roll. "Here comes your mother." Evvie nodded towards the far end of the cafeteria. There was Mom all right, heading straight for us. She was all business. It was hard going to school where my mom worked.

Mom gave Evvie a cool smile. "Hello, Evvie." I shook my head. Mom and Dad did not approve of Evvie or her mother because they were on welfare. I wished Mom liked my friend.

"Perk, I need you to take care of Bridey after school today. They've just called a late meeting. Marilyn has exams so she can't stay. You'll have to make dinner for Dad."

"Mom, Dad can watch Bridey! I have the festival, remember? Dad hates what I make for dinner anyway! Why can't he just throw a "Cranky Man" in the microwave?"

Evvie started laughing.

Mom didn't. Her mouth was tight and her nostrils were flared. I hated that look. "I'll see if Marilyn can stay an extra half hour, so you can make an appearance at the festival. I get a big argument whenever I ask you to help out! Quit eating all that junk," she snapped as she spun on her heel and left.

I was so mad I wanted to cry. She didn't have to

boss me around right there in the cafeteria. "Bitch," I said to her back.

Evvie was looking at me and folding her hard roll into bite size pieces. She had heard all of this before. I asked her, "Are you going to finish your chips?" I was starving all of a sudden. Evvie pushed what was left of the food over to me. "I should just come live with you," I said to Evvie in between bites.

"Okay, Priscilla, you can move in tonight. I'm sure your folks would just love that." She rolled her eyes at me. I had wanted her to say, "That would be great!" but she didn't.

Evvie grabbed my arm and pulled me towards the table reserved for the cool kids. Dom was one of them. "C'mon, let's hit the road." Evvie said.

"No, Evvie. I don't feel like it. I'll wait here." I hated being near those guys. She fit in, I didn't. They made me feel nervous and klutzy.

"Don't call me Priscilla." I said to her, but I was talking too quietly for her to hear, and she was too far away. My chest felt horrible. It wasn't just the bronchitis. I wanted to yell, but I couldn't do that. Actually, I wanted to scream and throw things. I hungrily finished the bag of chips and watched Evvie across the cafeteria.

She was talking to Dom. I could tell he was still in love with her and it made my chest ache even more. They went out last summer but Evvie broke up with him. They seemed to be teasing each other about something and Dom kept trying to grab Evvie's hand.

Now I felt irritated with Evvie too. Everything was bad, horrible, awful!

Dom met my eyes, and I froze. I wiped the Dorito dust off my face and I pretended I had bitten my lip. Oh my God! He was really looking at me!

I gave a tiny wave. I felt a tickle in my throat. Dom smiled and waved back. The tickle started turning into a small cough and I pressed my hand to my mouth. I managed to keep from coughing but instead let out a loud snort through my nose.

"Oh God! Please, not now!" I whispered. I could feel my face getting all red and weird. I started coughing, a loud jagged cough that sounded like a dying seal. I tried to turn away from Dom in a last ditch effort to disguise the fact that I was having a disgusting fit.

When I caught my breath, I looked back. I tried to smile and pretend nothing had happened. Kids were staring at me, so were the cafeteria ladies. Their stupid mouths were hanging open. Maybe they were scared the food had finally done someone in.

Dom was gone. Evvie was, too.

I didn't look at anyone as I left the cafeteria and headed outside towards the football field. The snow crunched under my feet.

"I deserve to freeze to death." I muttered.

I managed to keep from crying until I got past the bleachers. I didn't even care how cold it was without my jacket.

My jaw was clenched so tight it felt like it would

break. I muttered the whole way, "You are the grossest pig on the planet. Everyone hates you! You're fat and everyone will always hate you!"

When I found myself in the privacy of some pine trees, I started crying harder than I could ever remember. I pinched my gross doughy legs as hard as I could. The pain made me angry again. I could not remember ever being so angry. I'd show Mom, I'd show Dom, I'd show everyone. They would realize what a good person I was and feel sorry they weren't nicer to me.

"Why can't you just be like everybody else!" I growled. I wanted to scream the question into the cold air.

My ugly body had betrayed me and was always betraying me. The junk food swished around in my stomach. The blood pounded in my head.

Suddenly it all became clear. I knew what would make me feel better. I needed to relieve this pain in my stomach and my chest or I would explode into a thousand pieces of glass and ice. I looked around to make sure I was alone. I stuck my finger down my throat.

I made myself throw up.

Chapter 2

❖❖❖❖❖❖❖❖❖❖❖

What had started out to be my single most horrible, embarrassing day last winter turned out to be quite a learning experience. I thought I had discovered an excellent way to be able to eat as much as I wanted without gaining weight, but it didn't really work out that way.

I wondered whether a lot of people threw up. Maybe, and they just don't talk about it. It is kind of gross.

And, it does hurt, which can be a little scary. Sometimes a lot scary. Lately, I've been having a little trouble making it work right. I can't stand that. It's a vicious circle, because I get nervous if I can't get rid of everything I've eaten, and If I get too nervous I can't throw up. If I can't throw up, then I will get fat, then I'll have to move to Siberia, because there is nothing good nor happy on this planet for "chubby" girls.

Once it didn't work for some reason, so I tried using a spoon. I had read about that somewhere. It worked, except it was a little big for my throat and it got stuck. It felt like my throat just kind of clamped down on it. I remember thinking to myself, this is going to be sad. They are going to find me dead. I'll have this spoon sticking out of my mouth, and I'll still be all fat, because I didn't finish throwing up.

I managed to get it out, but I had to lie down on the ground and rest for a little while. I felt really dizzy and like I couldn't catch my breath. I was bleeding and everything.

I'm very careful that no one finds out that I make myself throw up. I don't want anyone to know. The only person who might suspect is Evvie. She caught me at the movies a few weeks ago. We had eaten a whole bunch of junk—candy, popcorn and nachos. Once I get started it's like I turn into a machine, and I can't stop eating. I can eat some pretty impressive amounts of food.

I went to the bathroom at a really good part in the movie where I didn't think anyone would leave. I kept flushing the toilet so no one would hear me throwing up. I didn't hear Evvie come in. She peered under the stall so she must have seen me sticking my finger down my throat.

"Perk, what are you doing? Are you all right?" She stood up and banged on the stall door so I had to let her in. She scared me to death. I was shaking so badly I could barely manage to get the toilet flushed and the door unlocked.

I was more angry than worried about getting caught because I needed to finish what I was doing before all that junk food started making me fat. She was already skinny. She didn't need to worry about the way she looked. It seemed selfish of her to butt in.

"I'm okay, Evvie, I just ate too much candy. It made me sick. You don't have to scare me!" I tried to sound kind of jokey, but I was still shaking.

"You looked like you were making yourself sick. You weren't, were you?" She rubbed my arm. I didn't appreciate the gesture of concern. I needed to hurry.

"Please! I've eaten something that made me sick. Hasn't that ever happened to you?" I tried to give her a quick little hug. I wished she would leave me alone. It also made me very uncomfortable to talk about what I had eaten, even if I was trying to throw her off the track. She was ruining everything! "Go back to the movie, I want to wash my face."

I'm not sure that she was convinced, but I pushed her out the door. All I could think about was that I didn't finish throwing up. I didn't finish, and now I'm going to get fat, and it will all be Evvie's fault, thin, pretty-as-a-model Evvie! She is as beautiful as any of those girls in the teen magazines. I look at those pictures and it makes me crazy. One day I will be able to fit into jeans and look like that. If I try really hard I can do it.

When she was gone, I tried to throw up the rest of

the food, but it didn't work. It wasn't something I could just start and then stop. I hated Evvie for that, I just hated her.

❖

We don't talk to each other now as much as we used to. She did ask me to stay over after school yesterday and help her babysit her little brother. I knew Mom was going to say no, she always does when Evvie is involved. I stopped by her office after lunch. She was glued to the phone, as usual.

"Uh-huh, uh-huh, yes, I understand Mrs. Jorgenson. The main thing is your son. Believe me, we'll find a way to work the whole thing out," said Mom. I tried to figure out who she was talking to. It always amazed me when I heard her solving other people's problems on the phone. She sounded like a completely different Mom. That just wasn't how she was with me. Both she and Dad always seemed angry at me, like I had somehow let them down when I was born.

I stared out the window while she finished her crisis call. Actually, it was nice to just sit for a minute and let my mind wander.

I circled my thumb and forefinger around my wrist. This was a great way to measure myself. If I could wrap them all the way around the bone of my wrist, things were great. If not, I knew I was being a pig and I had to crack down on my diet.

"Sweetie, what can I do for you? I'm very busy." Mom's long thin fingers rested on the phone pad. I loved her hands. Mine were red and stubby. The receiver was in her other hand. It was clear that she didn't have a whole lot of time.

"Mom, can I babysit at Evvie's tonight after school?" I felt a little breathless. I was in a hurry to get everything in.

"Not tonight, Hon," Mom said. She didn't think about it. She just said no.

"Why not? Why can't I ever go over there, Mom? She's my best friend and I keep having to make up excuses. I don't really feel right telling her, sorry, but my parents hate you."

"Perk, don't be so dramatic. We don't hate her. I'd just rather she came over to our house." Mom started shuffling through papers on her desk, as if she were looking for something. It made me mad that I was getting the "time's up" signal.

"Mom, please. She can't come over, she's babysitting. I think Evvie is getting tired of me because I'm never allowed to do any of the things she is." This was true. It was hard to keep making up excuses.

"There's a reason for that. It's because your father and I love you! I don't think I'm being completely fair to you, Perk. Sometimes I expect you to understand things you can't possibly be ready for yet! That girl is trouble. She doesn't care about you and she never will!"

I felt like Mom had slapped me in the face. I knew Evvie liked me, even if we weren't as close as we used to be. My chest started feeling all tight. "I can't believe you just said that! What a horrible thing to say!" I could feel my chin doing that trembly thing. I hated crying in front of other people, especially Mom. "Evvie does care about me!"

Mom jumped up and closed the door. "You listen to me, young lady," Mom put her face close to mine. I could smell her perfume. "First of all, you don't just stomp into my office and start hollering your head off like a two year old! You have no right to subject us all to your nasty moods. You will go right home after school! Are we clear on that?"

"Yeah, crystal clear. My plans mean nothing. I'm not the only one with nasty moods, and I'm not a two year old," I felt confused and angry. I was pretty sure I did have a right to be upset. Other people slept over at their friends' houses. Mom didn't need to be so mean. "I guess we're finished then!" I said, and stood up.

"You got it, kid." I don't know why she looked so angry. She had won.

She always did.

Things were closing in on me.

"I'm not coming over tonight, Evvie. Mom said no." I was following Dom and Evvie down the quiet hallway. I knew any minute a teacher would come around the corner and we would all get in trouble for roaming the halls. Dom and Evvie were walking arm in arm. It was driving me crazy. Evvie knew how I felt about Dom. Maybe Mom was right, maybe she didn't care about me. Or maybe, and this would be the pits, maybe they were getting together again.

"What's new?" Evvie waved her hand like she was dismissing me. "Come outside with us." She threaded her free arm through mine.

The three of us were linked. I peeked at Dom. He didn't appear to notice I had joined his little chorus line. It didn't matter, I was melting inside. Every part of me felt drippy and warm. I wished the bell would ring so everyone could see me arm in arm with Dominick Mazzola, even if Evvie was in the middle. I pretended she wasn't. I honestly considered stopping everything right there and explaining to Dom, calmly, cooly, and rationally, why he should just marry me, or at least learn my name.

We stopped in front of the heavy glass doors that led to the parking lot. Dom pushed one of them open with his big black boot. The sudden bright sunlight made me all squinty. Not one of my prettier faces.

"C'mon, Evvie, let's go." I jumped at the sound of Dom's voice. I had never really heard him talk that much. I wasn't usually this close to him. His voice wasn't as nice as the rest of him, kind of whiny and nasally. I guess it didn't matter. He was perfection in every other way.

Dom twirled his car keys around his finger. His hip was thrust out and his thick black hair was shining in the sunlight. He spun on his heel towards the parking lot.

"We're ditching school early," Evvie said. "I've got to get out of this hole."

I waited until Dom was out of earshot, "Evvie, do you like Dom again?" My heart was pounding.

"No. You are so dense! You're getting weirder and weirder, Perk. I know you have this 'till death do us part' thing for Dom. You might think about finding a boyfriend who knows you're alive, but I wouldn't get involved with him again without talking to you about it first."

I didn't know what was wrong with her. "It seems like you're really mad at me, Evvie. I don't understand." I felt the corners of my mouth pull down and my throat got tight.

Something bad was about to happen with us. I could feel it. I had felt it building and building since that night in the movie theater. Evvie kept asking me now if everything was okay. It was driving me nuts, because I haven't felt like talking a lot lately, except about stupid things. Every time I told her I was fine it seemed like she got madder and madder at me.

"You're right, I am upset with you. Lately you've been acting like you aren't even here. It's like you've gotten really stupid all of a sudden. I don't feel like I can talk to you anymore."

Evvie stuck her chin out at me. She looked a little

like she might cry. That almost made me happy. How dare she call me stupid and look so disappointed in me. She wasn't my mother!

Dom's car pulled up and he honked the horn. It wasn't his car, it was a midnight blue Mercedes that I had never seen. He revved the engine impatiently.

"Dom's waiting, Evvie. If you're done telling me what an idiot I am, you better go." I tried to look tough, but it didn't seem to be working. All I really wanted was for her to apologize and tell me we could forget the whole thing. Actually, I was feeling sort of blank and foggy. I tried to concentrate on Evvie's shoes.

Evvie tucked strands of her soft brown hair behind her ears. "Maybe you don't have time for a friend like me. You certainly don't seem to want to talk to me. Maybe you're not the person I thought you were," she said.

I tried to imagine who she thought I was.

Chapter 3

❖❖❖❖❖❖❖❖❖❖❖❖

I was still standing outside when the school bell rang. It sounded a thousand miles away. I watched Evvie and Dom tear off in the Mercedes. My arms and legs felt numb and heavy. I couldn't wait to get home so I could take a nap. A voice behind me made me jump.

"Are you studying the flora and fauna out here Perk, or do you have a class you're supposed to be in?" It was Mr. Blish, my science teacher. He was leaning on the glass door and shading his eyes from the light. He waved me inside. "I assume your friends had a pass to leave school property."

"I assume so." I liked Mr. Blish. He must be patrolling the hallways.

"Now that I've seen you in person, you will be in class later, right?"

"I assume so," I smiled at him. "I never skip your class. It's where I catch up on my sleep." I wished everyone in school was like him. I had art class this period. I stopped at my locker and got my artist's journal.

Ms. Bacharach was washing out paint jars and brushes in the sink. She always seemed genuinely glad to see me.

I had been taking private art classes from her since I was about nine years old. Once a year she took me to New York to a museum or an art show. Last year we went to the Guggenheim. It was the best time I had ever had. I felt like we were friends.

Ms. Bacharach handed me the brushes and eased herself onto a tall stool. She was seven months pregnant. I finished washing the brushes for her.

"I'm feelin' huge! I'm gettin' fat! And, I'm so tired!" She laughed and leaned on me. She did look pale.

"Oh, you look beautiful!" I laughed and patted her. I wondered if it bothered her to get so big. It would drive me nuts.

"You look upset, are you okay?" Ms. Bacharach stopped smiling and looked closely at me. She seemed to know when I wasn't feeling happy.

"I don't know. I had a little fight with Evvie and a big fight with my Mom." All of a sudden I felt like crying. I wished I was alone, or at least alone with Ms. Bacharach. I wanted her to hug me; actually, I wanted her to adopt me.

I wondered what she meant by not looking good. Did she mean fat? I wanted to ask but the bell rang. Ms. Bacharach gave me a squeeze and started class.

I hated feeling so emotional all the time. People were going to start thinking I was crazy. Maybe I was. Maybe I was one of those people you read about that just are never happy. I have an aunt like that. She lives in an institution in Poughkeepsie. We stopped visiting her years ago when she threw a pot of scalding coffee at Dad. She kept screaming at him to get out. He did, and we never went back. I pictured myself throwing coffee. I couldn't do it. Even if I was completely insane I don't think I would throw coffee. I would be a very well-behaved lunatic.

Bridey was still taking her afternoon nap when I got home. Marilyn was rushing around and collecting her things. "Your mom called, Perk. She's got another late meeting tonight. I put a lasagna in the oven." Marilyn bustled her way out the door. "Later, babes!" she called breathlessly and was gone.

"Yeah, bye," I waved. Everybody was zooming around living their lives, except me, Miss Available. Mom could have let me know I was going to be babysitting tonight. No wonder she wouldn't let me go to Evvie's.

Larry was sleeping with his belly on the heater vent. He loved to bake himself until he got so hot I was sure he would burst into flames. I pushed him over to make room for both of us. He gave me a lazy half lick that left his tongue attached to my arm.

"I know how you feel, Larry bear." I rubbed the velvety short black fur on Larry's nose and face. He was sound asleep again. The kitchen clock tick, tick, ticked on the mantle. It was that pre-twilight time of day that always made me chilly.

From my seat on the vent I could look through the glass balcony doors that led over the backyard. I studied the Esopus Creek at the bottom of our property. It was always noisy and swollen with melted snow in the springtime. I let my eyes get all blurry and stared at the last of the sun dancing on the surface of the water. I pulled Larry closer and wrapped my arms around his neck. Warmth radiated from the heater. I was ready to drift off to sleep.

"That's why we live here," Dad whispered, his voice was just behind my ear. He made me jump. He kneeled down on one knee next to me and stared out the window. "There's no place like the Catskills, Perk. Don't forget that." I looked at Dad. I had that feeling like I wanted to hug him again, but he stood up. He tossed his hat on the table and pulled a beer out of the fridge.

This was how I liked Dad. I loved when he talked about how pretty the mountains were. Sometimes he talked like I wanted to paint, with layers and layers. He could describe things and tell stories better than anyone I knew.

Other times he was like his coffee-throwing sister in Poughkeepsie.

He took a long swig of his beer and peeked into the oven, "What's the story? Is this thing done?"

"Almost, I'll get Bridey." I woke my little sister up and set her in her high-chair with a bagel to keep her quiet. Dad got tense when Bridey cried and fussed. Mom would always say to him, "Jack, she's just a baby," and smile. Then we'd all go into this big song and dance routine to keep Bridey occupied so she wouldn't make noise.

Bridey hummed the theme song from "Sesame Street" over and over. She dropped spoonfuls of lasagna on the floor.

The lasagna looked delicious, but I had decided not to eat dinner that night. Instead I nibbled on salad without dressing. I told myself to think about something else besides food. Dom popped into my head. That didn't help, it just made me nervous. I decided to have just a little piece of garlic bread.

"Why's she throwing her food on the floor?" Dad growled and tipped his head at Bridey. I could tell he was getting irritated. I wasn't really sure what to do, Bridey was just learning how to eat. I could see the tension rolling in like a thundercloud. I wondered about just taking Bridey back upstairs. We could finish dinner later.

Larry slid on his belly until he had managed to squeeze under the highchair where he could reach the lasagna on the floor. I forgot he was still inside. Very bad to forget that.

"Get that goddamned dog outside, Perk. For the millionth goddamned time, I don't want him in the kitchen while we're eating." Dad's voice was low and flat. He stopped stabbing his dinner with his fork and stared at his plate. My chest got tight.

I jumped up. "Larry, c'mon." I pulled him outside by his collar. Dangerous things had already been set in motion, this I knew. I wanted to change the subject and get Dad talking about something else.

"Hey, Dad! Maybe we could go for a little picnic at Balmer's Creek this weekend. It should be warm enough. Maybe Evvie could come." It was stupid to mention Evvie. It had just popped out of my mouth.

I sat back down at the table. Bridey had stopped singing, and was licking the butter off the top of her bread.

"No Perk," Dad tossed his napkin onto his plate. "Forget about Evvie. She's a waste of time. You should start trying to get hooked up with some new friends." Dad got up and took another beer out of the fridge. "Your mother and I talked about it. We don't want you hanging around with her anymore." He picked up a stack of unopened mail and headed for the living room.

I was stunned. "Excuse me just one second, Dad! You can't just say don't hang around her! She's my best friend!" I wanted to scream, "it's not fair!"

I had a horrible, angry feeling in my stomach. Bridey had her hands clamped over her ears and was crying. Her little wet face was bright red.

"You are way over the goddamned line, girl!" Dad moved across the room quickly, and knocked a kitchen chair over on its side. He backed me up against the sink.

He's going to kill me, I thought. I froze like a squirrel, right before it gets run over by a car. His face was in my face, and his eyes were slit and angry. His voice was low and tight. "You better remember whose house you're in because if you don't like my rules you can get your fat ass out." He backed off, picked up his beer, and disappeared into the other room.

My heart was pounding so hard I could hear it. Fat Ass! I wondered if it was possible for someone my age to have a heart attack. Everything looked weird, like it was slightly bent and a different color. I wondered how could he hate me so much. How could he hate his daughter so much? Was it because I was a fat ass?

I tried to catch my breath, but it felt like I was choking. I hated his moods! I hated him!

"Owies?" Bridey was crying. I wanted to scream at her to shut up, but I didn't.

"No owies, honey," I kissed her on the forehead. "We have an amazingly huge jerk for a father, though." I cleared the table, slamming chairs and dishes as I went.

Fat Ass! How dare he, I thought to myself. "Bridey, please stop crying!" I picked up bread from Bridey's plate and shoved it in my mouth, chewing and swallowing quickly. Everything inside me hurt. I just wanted to eat, to eat everything. I looked at all the leftover food on the table and got a weird feeling. It had been happening a lot lately. It's like

I go on automatic, and I get a whispering sound in my head. I don't like it, it sounds like a lot of little voices talking softly and so quickly that I can't figure out what they are saying. Every now and then I can make out the words "bad" and "Perk." It scares me. It makes me want to cry. It makes me want to hide.

I've noticed that if I eat when this whispering starts I don't hear it as much. I stuffed another piece of bread in my mouth. "Do you want ice cream, Bridey?" I asked my little sister. Bridey stopped crying and followed me to the fridge.

"Oooh! Strawberry!" I was still shaky. It helped to concentrate on the ice cream. I got two spoons, and hoisted Bridey onto my lap. I didn't bother with bowls. Bridey was humming again as she tried to get the ice cream to stay on her spoon with a pudgy little finger.

I stared off into space as I shoved one heaping icy spoonful after another into my mouth. I didn't chew, I just swallowed. It occurred to me from some dim, far off place that I had an ice cream headache.

That was okay. I felt better. Mom and Dad and Evvie had almost become the last things on my mind.

I wondered vaguely what I should do with Bridey while I made myself throw up.

Chapter 4

❖❖❖❖❖❖❖❖❖❖❖❖

I was in a bathroom stall at school. It was freezing. The light was strange, thin and yellow. The hairs on the back of my neck were standing up.

Footsteps echoed off of the tiled walls. Black patent leather shoes stopped outside my door. They faced me, the tips of the shoes were on my side of the stall. They were small shoes, child-sized. I had seen this girl before. She had been visiting me in nightmares for weeks.

I scrunched as high up as I could on the back of the toilet. I put my feet up on the rim in hopes that I would remain hidden. I was sure the pounding in my chest was as loud as thunder.

"Who's there! Go away!" I croaked. My breath escaped in small, blue puffs. The child stood outside, waiting, silent. I couldn't take my eyes off of the patent leather shoes.

The stall door slowly opened, as if it had never been locked. I leaned on the door with all my might, but the child was very strong. Wake up, Perk, I told myself. I heard voices, whispering, whispering. The child peered around the door at me. Her face and hair were a sickly yellow. Her mouth was fixed open with ragged teeth. Her eyes were light blue with catlike pupils, and when I looked into them I saw death. The creature stared at me and put her hand on my chest. She pushed, slowly and steadily. I started to fall, the toilet was in my way and I couldn't get my balance. She kept pushing and I started to cry. She was going to hurt me, and I didn't know how to make her stop.

"Mom! Mom!" I woke up yelling. My face was wet. I wanted Mom right now, but I was too afraid to get out of bed. It took a minute to realize that the pale, gray light seeping through my curtains meant it was early morning.

I heard Moonpie running on his wheel. I hugged my pillow to my chest. I could still feel the nightmare girl's breath on me, and my hair felt electrified.

"Mommy..." I opened my bedroom door and tiptoed out to the stairs. I heard Mom talking to Bridey in the kitchen. I went back to bed and lay down nose to nose with Larry.

"Do you love me, Larry?" He licked my face.

"Something's happening to me, but I don't know what it is!" I felt like I had oceans of tears hiding behind my face. Maybe I would go downstairs and tell Mom that I had been feeling really bad lately. Maybe I could somehow tell her about throwing up, but I knew I didn't want to tell Mom about that.

I rubbed my neck. My sore throat reminded me that I threw up again last night.

"I can't do that anymore. I'm going to be very good today. I'll only drink water and eat fruit." I felt a little better after deciding to turn over a new leaf.

I took Moonpie out of his cage and rubbed his warm little body against my cheek. I wondered if Dad had told Mom that he had called me a fat ass last night. Probably not.

I stretched out on the floor and let the little mouse sit on my stomach. His black eyes sparkled as he washed his whiskers. He was looking at me. I wished he could tell me what he was thinking. Animals knew things that people couldn't possibly understand.

Mom sat at the kitchen table, stirring her coffee. She looked tired. Bridey was on the floor with all of her toys spread around her.

"Tough morning?" I asked Mom.

"Don't even ask. Thank God it's Saturday. Otherwise I'd be dead on my feet today. Your friend Rosy called when I got home last night, but I told her you were asleep."

"Rosy! What in the world did she want?" Rosy

Wenner was an ex-best friend of mine from about a billion years ago. Her father was my dad's boss. I avoided her at school and only saw her when she traveled with her dad to the job sites. Mom loved her.

"She's going to stop over this afternoon while her dad picks up some paperwork. I told her that would be fine."

"Mom! We're not friends anymore. You could have told her I'd call her back." I poured myself a cup of coffee.

"Perk, you're not allowed to have coffee!" Mom said. "Rosy is a good influence on you. If you live through the visit you might just find you have fun. It would beat sneaking cigarettes and everything else you and Evvie do together."

"Not anymore, thanks to you and Dad. Dad broke the big news to me last night about Evvie being off limits. That really sucks, Mom." I was getting angry again, and the sun was barely up. I poured out the coffee in the sink and slammed the cup down. The noise startled me.

"Can't you think of a better word than 'sucks,' Perk? I can't seem to get you to speak like you have a brain!" Mom threw her coffee spoon down on the kitchen table. It bounced off and clattered to the floor. Bridey looked up with a start.

"Maybe I'm too fat assed to think of another word besides 'sucks!' It seems like a good word right now!" I kicked the kitchen wall, hard. I was only wearing socks, so it hurt.

"Priscilla Sinclair! Quit swearing!" Mom yelled. Bridey remained on the floor, her head turning back and forth as if she were following a tennis match.

"But Dad called me a fat ass last night!" I kicked the wall again. It still hurt.

Mom pushed me back from the wall. "Don't kick that, please. Why did Dad say that to you? What did you do?" Mom stopped yelling.

"I don't know, nothing!" I started crying. I could feel my face getting more and more swollen. I was a big crying blob. "It really hurt my feelings, Mom."

Mom sighed and shook her head. "Perk, you know how he can be. He doesn't mean it when he says that stuff. You know that he loves you." She hugged me. I felt limp. Mom was wrong. I didn't really know Dad loved me. That made me cry even more.

"I don't feel good," I said. I wanted to tell Mom about how I just didn't like myself much anymore. "Do you think I'm a fat ass?"

"No. Quit asking me that. I don't like that language. I didn't think you were fat before, Honey. I said chubby."

"I weigh a lot less now Mom, I was 140 pounds before I got bronchitis last winter," I said.

"Oh my God, Perk. You were? I've never in my life weighed 140 pounds!" Mom looked as if she had just been slapped. I felt my face get hot and red.

"It wasn't really that much, I just rounded it up." I wished Mom would stop staring at me. All of a sudden I felt like I had a huge battleship attached to my rear end and thighs that I would have to maneuver up to my room under Mom's scrutiny.

"So, am I fat now?" I laughed a fake laugh. I wanted to know more than anything else in the world.

"Oh Perk! What is the matter with you! I thought we were talking about Rosy."

"I thought we were talking about Dad." I refilled my coffee cup, leaving to take a shower.

"Nothing is as bad as you think, Perk," Mom yelled after me, "and dump out that coffee!"

I felt the tears behind my face again. An intense headache was threatening to start.

If nothing is as bad as I think, I wondered, then why do I feel like I'm losing my mind?

Chapter 4

❖❖❖❖❖❖❖❖❖❖❖

I decided to get some painting done before Rosy showed up. Whenever I worked, there was no confusion and things felt right. I opened my windows and let in the cool spring air. The Esopus sounded clean and healing. I pulled my easel over to the window so I could use the morning light. I painted for a few hours, until Larry jumped off my bed, and ran downstairs.

"Perk! Rosy's here!" Mom called.

"Big deal," I muttered to myself.

I took my time getting downstairs. Rosy was carrying a little cage with a few black and white mice.

"Why did you bring your mice?" I asked.

"Hello to you too, Miss Sunshine," Rosy said with a big, geeky smile. I don't know why she liked me so much. It irritated me. "I thought Moonpie would like to meet some new friends."

"Well, I don't think he does." I poked my finger

through the wire bars. One of the little mice looked up to investigate. He looked more ratish than Moonie.

"Let's go upstairs and introduce them." Rosy bounded up the stairs.

I noticed she was a little fatter than the last time I had seen her. It made me glad. I poked my hipbone.

I followed her up to my room.

Rosy was looking at my bedroom walls. "I still think you're a great artist, Perk. Someday you're going to be famous."

"Yeah, right." I was being sarcastic, but I loved it when people told me they liked my work.

Rosy set the mouse cage on the floor and flopped onto my bed. "You look weird. Are you sick?"

"What do you mean, weird?" It took her no time at all to get on my nerves.

"Like puffy or tired or something. No big deal." She put on my old bathrobe and batted her eyes at me like she was some crazy actress.

"How could I look puffy? I've lost weight!"

"I don't know, Perk. Forget it. You look great!" Rosy gave me another smile. I wished she would just say what she meant.

"Can't you stop being an idiot for a minute? Maybe you could tell me I look good instead of telling me I look puffy, unless I do! Do I?" I could hear my voice getting shrill. Rosy wasn't smiling any more.

"Don't call me an idiot. I didn't realize I was supposed to give you a big gold ribbon for losing a few pounds. It's not like you're fat, Perk," Rosy said.

"Well, why is everyone talking to me about how much I weigh!" I wasn't sure why I was yelling at Rosy, or what I was yelling about at all.

"Tell them to shove it! Not everyone looks like your supermodel friend, Evvie. The rest of us are normal. Anyway, Evvie isn't as nice as you, and she isn't an artist. I'd rather be you any day." Rosy put her arm around me and gave a squeeze. "Remember when we used to pretend we were beautiful, famous movie stars and we'd go to parties and everyone loved us? I guess it turns out we're just regular people."

I looked at Rosy and sniffed. It felt okay to be hugged. "You don't have the same problem, so you don't understand, Rosy. Everybody likes you. Your mom and dad like you. My mom and dad love you! Mom's always talking about what 'smarts' you have. She says you're 'perky.' I think she wishes you were her very own Perky and that I would join the army or something."

Rosy laughed. "Everyone likes you too, Perk. Besides, look at me, and tell me I don't have the same problem. I'm short and I'm covered with freckles. Just compare your nice straight hair to my black frizz. God!"

"Really?" I looked in the mirror. Sometimes I did look okay. I circled my fingers around my wrist. I could be thinner, that's all. That would fix everything.

"Really. So can we stop talking about you now? Let's introduce our mice."

Rosy turned and caught her elbow on Moonpie's

cage. I saw Moonpie arch his back as his feet left the ground. I leapt forward to try and break the fall, but I was too far away.

"Oh my God!" I pushed Rosy out of the way. Moonpie was caught between the flat metal base and the wire wall of the cage. His tongue was swollen. His small body was twitching. I couldn't breathe.

"Oh Perk, I'm so sorry! I'm so sorry! Is he okay?" Rosy dropped to her knees next to me. I pushed her away, hard.

"Get off of me!" I didn't know what to do. I picked up Moonpie and cradled him in my hand. "Get my mom." It scared me the way his eyes were fixed. His tongue looked like a tiny pink balloon.

"I'll be right back. I'm so sorry. It was an accident." Rosy turned and ran down the stairs. I could hear her crying as she called for Mom and her dad.

"Moonie, Moonie, please don't die." I tried to blink away the hot tears so I could focus on my little friend. "I love you!" Sadness and anger filled my chest and spread down my arms. It was such a big, achy feeling, such a bad feeling.

Rosy's father came into my room with Mom. "I know a good way to tell if your little guy is going to make it. We'll do the old whiskey test. Bring him over here."

I was not surprised when Rosy's father produced a silver liquor flask from his back pocket. I had seen her Dad performing the 'whiskey test' on himself many times. He poured a drop of the amber liquid onto a calloused finger and touch the mouse's tongue. Moonpie did not react. My heart sank.

"That doesn't look too good, kiddo. Normally, the booze would get him to kick a bit. I'm sorry. I'll put him out of his misery if you like." Rosy's father stood up and put his big meaty hand on my shoulder.

"No! No, please, just go. Thanks." I looked at Mom and felt my face screw up with tears.

"I'm sorry, Honey. I'll be downstairs, okay?" Mom closed the door behind them as they filed out, leaving me alone.

My eyes felt like I had been swimming in chlorine all day. I had never had anything I loved die before. I wished I could turn back the clock and lock Rosy out of the house. If I had put my foot down with Mom, Moonie would be okay.

"Thanks for being my friend, Moonie." I kissed him on the ear. His body was still and I knew he was dead. I looked away.

I dumped out my jewelry box and lay Moonpie in it. I covered him with a tissue. I untacked a small pencil portrait I had done of myself from the wall and put it in the box, along with his food dish. I tried to put his exercise wheel in, but it wouldn't fit. I wished Mom had stayed upstairs with me. I wasn't sure if I was supposed to say a prayer or what.

I felt like I was floating. I pulled a red scarf off my bureau and tied it around my head. I imagined that I was on my way to Moonpie's funeral, and everyone was there, Evvie, Dom, Dad. They all felt badly that

I had lost one of my best friends. I could picture Dom coming over to me, and taking my hand. He would say something like, "I'm so sorry for your loss." He would fall in love with me because I was so strong, despite being in so much pain.

I went downstairs and took one of Dad's flannel workshirts out of the hall closet. Rosy and her dad were gone.

"You shouldn't be too hard on Rosy, Perk. She felt really bad." Mom held Moonpie's makeshift coffin while I put the red and black jacket on.

"Gee, that's too bad. I hope she's going to be okay," I said, and walked out the door.

The afternoon clouded over. I was glad for Dad's jacket. I jog-walked to the woods that butted up against our property. Larry ran to catch up and take the lead. He looked sad. I knew he understood what had happened to our friend.

I got to a perfect spot and stopped at the edge of the water. I thought of one of my favorite paintings. It was called *Le Jeune Martyr*. It showed a beautiful maiden with long, wavy, golden hair like a princess and a peaceful look on her face. She was dead, floating in the water. I remembered how pretty she had looked, how calm.

I wondered if I would look that way if I was floating in the water. Probably not. But I knew it would sure be a lot more peaceful than what was happening now. Maybe something could happen where I could almost drown, something that left me looking good like the girl in the painting.

I wondered if Dom would visit me in the hospital. I imagined him stroking my feverish head. I would be in a coma, incredibly beautiful, and incredibly thin from being on an I.V. for so long. The nurses would tell him, "We don't know why she's still alive, she must be hanging on for true love." He would kiss me back to health, and then marry me, immediately.

I slipped and my sneaker slid into the water. It was icy cold, and sent an instant crampy feeling up the back of my leg. Larry whimpered and barked.

"Hush up, Larry. Let's get to work." I brushed the wet pine needles and dirt aside. I had forgotten to bring something to dig with. "Damn. Now what am I going to do?" I didn't want some woods creature, or Larry, to get into the jewelry box. Larry barked again and ran off into the woods, kicking up muddy dirt.

"Larry! You pain!" I called, but I was afraid. I couldn't hear anything this close to the big noisy creek, but I knew that Larry could.

Something came crashing towards me. I crouched down and backed myself into the weeds hoping to make myself smaller. If I ran, whatever it was would surely see me and catch me. It was better to hide. I hid my face in my hands. I expected the demon girl from my dreams to pounce on me at any moment.

"There you are! I've been waiting for you." It was Dom.

Chapter 6

❖❖❖❖❖❖❖❖❖❖❖

Dom! I would have been less surprised to see a herd of reindeer crashing through the trees. I ripped the old red scarf off my head. "What are you doing here?"

Dom shook his glossy black curls out of his eyes and shifted his weight. He smiled at me, at least I think he was smiling.

I tried to smile back. Dom had never really even said more than hello and now here he was in my woods, at my house. I heard a small voice in my head, warning me to be careful.

"What's that?" He gestured with his head to the jewelry box.

Suddenly I felt embarrassed by the funeral I was holding for my little friend. It seemed childish. "It's my baby sister's dead mouse. I was going to bury it for her."

"Yeah? How about a Viking funeral. We can do it

right here." Dom took a lighter out of his pocket. My head felt thick and foggy as I watched him try to light the box. I knew this was all wrong but I was afraid he would leave if I told him to stop.

"Dom! Wait. You know, I really should wait for my sister. It was her mouse and everything," I whispered. When flames began to lick the side of the cardboard, he hooted gleefully and tossed it into the Esopus.

I betrayed my little Moonpie. I watched the now open box dance in and out of the whitewater as it rushed downstream.

"I'm sorry, Moonpie," I whispered and pressed my fingers into my eyes to prevent more tears. I was starting to wish Dom would leave.

He lit a cigarette. "That's how I want to go. My old man says it's supposed to bring good luck, or something." He flashed me another smile. I saw a piece of tobacco on his front tooth.

"Really?" I was watching his face. It bothered me that his eyes didn't smile with his mouth. I had never noticed that before. I heard that little voice again.

"So listen, I have something you can help me with," Dom said, and grabbed my hand! It felt warm, soft, and amazingly great. I forgot about Moonpie until Dom pulled me through the prickly brambles.

I took a final look over my shoulder towards the water. Larry met my eyes. He looked like he was saying, "How could you let him do that to Moonpie?"

"I'm kind of surprised you came to me for help,

Dom, but I'll do whatever I can."

"Yeah, that's what I figured." He led the way through the overgrown path. It was slippery from the spring thaw. Larry pushed past me on the path to avoid the snapping branches.

We came to a small clearing in the woods. I saw the midnight blue Mercedes that Dom had been driving around. He had pulled it in as far as it would go without becoming stuck in the mud and fallen trees.

"Well, here she is." Dom said proudly. He spread his arms out as if he was presenting a prize on a television game show.

For a second I wondered if he meant he was giving it to me. "I don't get it."

Dom smiled at me again. I was getting a very bad feeling about this car. "Actually, I sort of came across it illegally, and I need to stash it here for a little while, okay? Someone told me the police know I have it."

My father's face flashed into my head bigger than life, then I imagined policemen, then gunfire, then me, in jail.

"You mean you stole it?" I couldn't take my eyes off the car. "Dom, I don't think you should leave it here. Whose is it?"

"I don't know. It had been sitting behind Kirk's Market for awhile. I figured it must have been ditched. There's one other thing." Dom walked around to the rear of the car. I could tell by the ruined metal that somebody had forced their way in. He opened the trunk. "*Voila!*"

I peered carefully into the dark space and felt the hair on my arms prickle. There was an automatic rifle. Upstate New York is full of hunters and I had seen many rifles, but never an automatic gun. I was afraid of Dom all of a sudden.

"I-I-I think you have to take all of this away," I stammered. I hoped he wouldn't get angry and shoot me. I was staring at him.

"What are you being so weird about? No one would even see the car except you. I wanted to show you so you wouldn't find it sitting here and tell your parents. Evvie said you would be cool about it!"

"Evvie!" Now he was lying, I knew it. I was beginning to forget why I ever thought Dom was so great anyway. He was acting completely creepy.

"Evvie said you'd do anything for me. I guess she was wrong. You don't seem cool at all. In fact, you seem supremely uncool."

I couldn't think of anything to say. I wanted someone to tell me what to do.

"Maybe you could leave it farther downstream," I offered, trying to sound optimistic. I watched his face get dark and angry. I kept hoping that the "good" Dom would make an appearance and save the day.

Dom sneered at me. The tobacco flake had moved to another tooth. "Yeah, right. Thanks for nothin' Sinclair." Dom strutted over to the car and angrily pulled the door open. He gunned the engine, releasing a cloud of blue smoke, and maneuvered the car back through the trees without looking at me.

I stood still and stared at the tire marks in the mud where the car had been. I felt flat, beyond tears. A shiver ran up my spine.

Moonpie popped into my head. The thought of him and his open coffin in the freezing water made my stomach turn.

I hurried back to the house to get my bike. I could ride into town and go to Brio's coffeeshop and eat. I figured I deserved this. After all, my mouse had just died, and my make-believe boyfriend was a criminal.

I took the stairs two at a time up to my room. I grabbed my big sweater and yanked a brush through my hair.

I caught a glimpse of myself in the mirror. I looked like I was crying, but I wasn't. My eyes were tired and smudgy, and sad. I swallowed all of the feelings down. I didn't have time to feel sorry for myself. I needed to eat.

I grabbed my backpack and ran downstairs. I thought about the menu at Brio's. I had to eat soft things, easy things to throw up. I usually ordered a big gooey cheese omelet and muffins, and of course, a big vanilla shake.

Mom was in the kitchen, cutting vegetables. Dad was back from work early. I could tell Mom had mentioned the "fat ass" remark. Dad wouldn't look at me while he washed his hands at the sink.

"Where did you bury your mouse, Hon?" Mom asked. Dad stayed silent.

"In the woods. I have to go into town and get some stuff for a project." I didn't feel like talking about Moonpie.

"Be back before dark," Dad said in a deep, deliberate voice. He kept washing his hands and didn't turn around.

"Right," I said and ran outside. I buttoned my jacket and jumped on my bike.

I coasted across Route 28 and rode the short distance into town.

Phoenicia, N.Y. was so small that I could ride from one end of town to the other in thirty seconds, less if there was no cross traffic. I chained my bike in Brio's coffeeshop parking lot and hurried inside.

I sat at the counter and ordered. There was a little plastic basket of saltines on the table. I ate the entire basket, and replaced the crumpled cellophane. Waiting for my eggs was excruciating. I couldn't get comfortable. It felt too warm. I felt like everyone in the restaurant was watching me. I reached in my backpack and pulled out a tattered paperback. I needed to fix my eyes somewhere.

The waitress set down my omelet. I picked up my fork and looked around the restaurant nervously. It was fairly full. I froze when I saw Loretta Gauthier, a friend of my parents. I hid my face behind the book.

I wolfed every bit of food on my plate in a few minutes. I ordered a piece of cake to go, "for my little sister at home." After I paid my check, I went across the street to Kirk's Market and bought powdered donuts, two ice cream sandwiches, and a yogurt drink. "I got elected to do the food run for my study group," I said and fake smiled. I ate one donut at a time as I walked so that no one would notice how much I was eating. I washed each bite down with the yogurt drink.

My stomach pressed against my waistband, and I had to unbutton my pants. My head felt too big for my body and I had an urge to lie down. Eating made me feel much better, but being so full made me feel horrible.

I walked quickly towards Phoenicia Park. It was off the main drag and people wouldn't be hanging out there until it was warmer outside. I knew I would have some privacy.

I walked to the far end of the small park. It was completely empty. My temples were throbbing and I was having a hard time breathing. I picked a spot at the edge of the woods. I took my rubberband out of my pocket and tied my hair back. I jammed my fingers down my throat. I was so used to cutting my knuckles on my teeth that I didn't even feel it anymore. I threw up.

"Cookie! Cookie, you pest!" A voice called in the distance. I frantically tried to find my wet wipes in my bag. I knew who Cookie was—Loretta Gauthier's Jack Russell terrier. My knees felt weak. I couldn't find anything to wipe my hands and face off with.

"Cookie, do you really have to torment everyone?" Loretta laughed. She sounded much closer.

To my horror, Cookie appeared at my feet. I knew

Loretta would be close behind. He barked hello, and then became very interested in the mess that I was trying to cover with leaves.

"Get out of here, Cookie!" I growled, and pinched him in the rear. He yipped, looked at me with his little head cocked, and went back to nosing in the leaves.

"Hi, Loretta!" I called and tried to sound cheerful.

"Perk, what a surprise! Oh, no, are you sick to your stomach?" she asked. This was one of those times I wished I could snap my fingers and stop the action until I had figured out what to do.

"I ate something bad. I think I need some privacy." I said. I looked down and saw my pants were still unbuttoned. Smooth.

"Well, I can't leave you out here if you're ill. Honey. I'll give you a ride home." Loretta stepped towards me. I took a step backwards.

"Really, Loretta. I'm okay." I could still feel food in my stomach, and I knew with every passing second I was getting fatter and fatter. I needed to finish.

"Perk, I don't mean to pry. I noticed you at the coffeeshop and then eating stuff at Kirk's. Why are you getting sick all the way out here in the park?" Loretta waited for me to say something.

"What kind of a question is that?" I picked up my backpack and walked quickly across the patchy grass.

Loretta ran to keep up with me. "I wasn't spying, Perk. My friend was getting groceries at Kirk's. I was waiting outside. If it wasn't for Cookie I wouldn't even have seen you here."

There was a chorus of voices in my head chanting, "She knows, you're snagged, she's going to tell your parents!" I tried to push them and Loretta out of my head so I could figure out a place to finish.

"Listen, Perk, I used to eat and throw up every day, several times a day. You look just like I used to. Your throat is swollen, your stomach is distended..."

I stopped and glared at Loretta. Maybe if I payed attention to her for a minute she would shut up and leave me alone. She sighed and planted her fists on her hips.

"I ended up in the hospital, and they even took my daughter away for a while. It was the worst time in my life. You have to be very, very careful. It's called bulimia..."

"Duh! I go to school. I know what that is!" I pushed past Loretta. My heart was pounding. I couldn't believe she said my stomach was distended. It was her fault I hadn't finished throwing up!

"You need to talk to someone. I'm going to be worried about you, Perk." Loretta grabbed my wrist.

I yanked my arm away from her. "Well don't worry! Just leave me alone!"

I walked quickly back to Brio's where I had left my bike. I had a bad cramp in my side.

I pedaled hard all the way home, and tried to calculate how many calories and grams of fat were left in my stomach. Now the voices were singing, "You're fat! You're fat!"

Loretta had ruined everything! I wanted to scream.

I was not going to eat one single bite of food except diet soda from now until tomorrow night. Maybe longer. If I rode my bike to school tomorrow that would help burn off some extra calories. In fact, it would probably be a good idea to ride my bike to school every day.

I was home in a few minutes. I leaned my bike against the house and ran upstairs. I grabbed the back of my jeans to see if they were really as tight as they felt.

I heard Mom and Bridey in the nursery. Bridey was singing off key. I stopped by her room. Mom was standing on a chair and hanging an oversized alphabet on the wall. She was humming the ABC song.

"Hi!" Bridey squealed. "Perkie!" She ran to me with her arms wide open. I dropped to my knees and squeezed my sister.

"Hi, little sugarpop." My heart swelled. I rubbed my nose against the baby's soft cheek. "I'm going to bed, Mom. I don't feel good."

Larry was asleep on my bed. I shoved him over, kicked off my shoes, and pulled the blankets up to my chin. It was going to be weird going to sleep without the sound of Moonpie's squeaky wheel. I could try to throw up now, but it was too late. I knew I had absorbed much of the food and it was on its way to do its dirty work. I imagined the picture of the circulatory system that hung on my wall in science class. I pictured greasy globules of omelets and donuts coursing through my blood, through my arteries, on the way to my legs, my butt, and my stomach. I kicked my feet under the blanket. Damn Loretta!

What I couldn't quite keep out of my head was what would happen if Loretta decided to talk to Mom and Dad. I was having a hard time figuring out how I would explain I had been throwing up.

I didn't really understand it myself.

Chapter 7

❖❖❖❖❖❖❖❖❖❖❖

The thought of seeing Dom on Monday morning was making me nervous. I decided the best tactic would be to pretend nothing had happened this weekend.

There was a card folded into the slots of my locker. My heart jumped in hopes that it might be from Dom. I had to keep reminding myself that he had turned out to be a creep.

It was from Rosy. I tossed it back into the locker. I didn't care how sorry she was, I would never speak to her again.

"Hi, Perk." I was surprised to see Loretta's daughter, Nicole. Nicole was a twelfth grader. She handed me a manila envelope.

"What's this?" I asked. After the episode with Loretta yesterday, I suspected this envelope would be trouble.

"Dunno, Mom said to give it to you." Nicole gave

me a little wave before disappearing into the sea of kids on their way to class. I stared at the envelope. Things were definitely falling apart. I didn't seem to be able to control anything anymore, and that made me feel crazy.

I threw the mystery envelope on top of the card from Rosy and slammed the locker shut. Everyone was totally bugging me.

I rubbed my throbbing head. I had woken up starving in the middle of the night last night. I went downstairs to find a low fat snack and instead ended up eating a whole loaf of raisin bread with butter and honey.

I always tasted blood when I threw up these days. It scared me. I was worried that I might be giving myself cancer or something.

In the morning, Mom was looking for the missing raisin bread, but I told her it had gotten moldy. Even though Mom counselled kids my age, she never seemed to have a clue about what was going on with me.

I decided to skip my first period class and find Ms. Bacharach. I walked the now empty hallway toward the art rooms.

There was a figure in the distance, and I knew it was Evvie. She held her books tight against her chest and the muted ceiling lights made the soft fluff of her hair look like a halo. I couldn't see her face.

"Hi, Evvie!" I called. She didn't answer. The first thought that popped into my head was that she didn't like me anymore.

"You should have just called me about that stupid car, Perk. I could have fixed it so you didn't look so lame in front of Dom. It was really no big deal."

I felt like I got caught doing something wrong. "Why are you mad at me? Did Dom bother to tell you there was a gun in the car?" My lower lip was trembling.

"What did you think he was going to do, shoot you?" She stared at me for a minute, her eyes looked distant. "Anyway, it doesn't matter, I have to go." Evvie turned to leave.

"Evvie, I guess I got weirded out...let's go to the cafeteria." I pulled on her arm.

"I don't think so, Perk. You seem so messed up lately. I don't have time to be a mind reader and figure out what's going on with you. It's too tiring." She pulled her arm away from me and left.

"Evvie," I croaked, but she kept walking.

I walked quickly toward the bathroom and ducked into the stall. I didn't want to cry. I swallowed everything up and felt my face and heart turn to stone. I sat on the toilet. It seemed that I should keep moving or I might become completely paralyzed. I rocked back and forth and stared blankly at some red magic marker on the wall that said "Betty Barnett does it all night long."

I dug my nails into the palms of my hands. I needed to feel something else besides sickness and confusion. I bit my fingertip and tried to draw blood. I deserve to hurt, I thought angrily, and bit myself again. I wanted relief. My body felt like a prison.

I threw open the stall door. A girl leaning over the sink with a mascara wand in one hand and a cigarette in the other jumped and looked at me.

"Hey! You made me mess up!" the girl exclaimed.

"Sorry." I said. I wondered if the girl could see that I was having a nervous breakdown. Probably not, I was pretty good at hiding how I felt.

I went to Ms. Bacharach's classroom and ducked into the small storeroom that she used as an office. I saw the clay paperweight that I'd given her as a Christmas gift when I was nine years old. That seemed like a lifetime ago.

"Perk, is that you?" Ms. Bacharach poked her head around the door.

"I feel really bad." I stared at the ground. Something was going to happen. I could feel it in my chest, in my face, in my jaw. I had to tell someone what was happening because I knew if I didn't I would splinter into a thousand pieces.

"What do you mean, honey?" She closed the door. It was hard to fit a pregnant Ms. Bacharach and me in the room at the same time.

"Something's wrong with me." I couldn't look at my teacher. She waited for me to say more.

"Are you hurt? Did something happen?" Ms. Bacharach laid her hand over mine. I was surprised how cold and clammy it felt.

I loved Ms. Bacharach, but I didn't want her to touch

me. It made me feel afraid, like I was doing the wrong thing by talking to her. Dad had always said there was nothing that I couldn't handle if I put my mind to it. I thought of Mom. She would hate people knowing that there was something wrong with her daughter.

I pulled my hand away. The storeroom was hot and claustrophobic. "Never mind, maybe I'm getting my period or something." Another secret is I stopped having my period almost a year ago, which also made me think I had some terminal disease. I made a goofy "duh" noise and rolled my eyes. I pulled my shirt away from my skin, and felt little rivulets of perspiration. I was seconds away from sweating to death.

"Perk, you can tell me what's wrong. I'll try and help you." Ms. Bacharach reached for my hand again, but I pulled away.

"I'm okay, really, I'm fine." I smiled and slid out of the room. I took a deep breath in the hallway and decided to go to the cafeteria.

I stacked my tray with a cheeseburger, two bags of potato chips, a grilled cheese with bacon, and a slice of apple pie. I asked for tin foil to wrap everything. I prayed no one I knew would come in and see me with all of this food. I explained to the cafeteria ladies that I had been elected to do "lunch duty" for my friends, that's why I had ordered so much. In fact, I told them cheerfully, I wouldn't even be eating since I had just started a new diet.

I told myself to shut up, they don't care.

I put the food in my backpack, and headed for the

auditorium. It was empty. I picked a seat where I could see everything.

I poked myself after every few bites, to see if I was getting fatter. The class bell rang. I slunk lower in my seat, and sharp pains shot through my stomach.

I started to cry, for a moment, and then went back to my food.

I smoothed my hair back and took a deep breath. Standing up straight was hard because I hurt from being so full. I wanted to hide my big fat belly and get to the girl's bathroom, where it was fairly safe to throw up as long as classes were in session.

I lifted the rim of the toilet and pushed my fingers down my throat. Every thing felt disconnected all of a sudden and I wondered why I heard people singing in the bathroom. A sickening grayness crept in at the side of my eyes, and I started to fall.

I heard a school bell in the soupy distance and a voice in my head screamed GET UP! The door shot open and the bathroom filled with girls. I had fainted.

"Oh gosh!" I whispered, and forced my shaking hands to flush the toilet. I dug in my backpack for the wet wipes, but nothing in my bag was making sense to me. Names of things clogged my head, brush, notebook, but they didn't have any meaning.

Vomit had dried on my hands. I had never fainted before. If I was dying, I hoped it wouldn't happen until I got home. I didn't want anyone at school to find me.

"It stinks in here! Open a window!" I heard a voice yell. I took a deep breath to steady myself and left the bathroom stall.

"Pee-eeww! Do you want the nurse?" A girl asked.

"It was someone else!" I said. The girl shrugged and stamped out her cigarette on the floor.

❖

I decided to go to the school library to read something about bulimia. Just because I was going to look didn't mean anything. I needed to figure out the difference between bulimia and what I had been doing.

I picked a book at random under "EATING DISORDERS" in the card catalog and quickly pushed the drawer shut. I didn't want anyone to see what I was looking for. I found the book and stared at it for a minute before taking it down from the shelf. I sat cross legged on the floor, alone in the aisle, and opened the book.

I scanned the case study of a bulimic girl named "Mary." Except for a few things it was my story, my feelings. She even heard voices like I did. It was weird, I felt kind of invaded. I didn't like to say the word, bulimia. It sounded fat and weak.

I still didn't know what to do. Was I supposed to tell people? I didn't want to do that.

I saw some kids run past the aisle. I went back to the book and tried to concentrate on the rest of Mary's story. My chest got tight when I started reading about therapy, hospitals, and doctors. This wasn't possible for me, no way. I wasn't even sure that I didn't want to be bulimic. I just wanted to feel better, and stop being such a pig.

I heard an ambulance siren. It sounded like it was just outside. A few more kids ran by my aisle. I slipped the book back into its place on the shelf and went to investigate. Everyone in the library was pushing to get to the window that looked out over the front of the school.

I stood on a chair and glimpsed a paramedic opening an ambulance door as a stretcher was brought to the van. The figure on the stretcher gripped the paramedics arm. The blanket was covered with ominous looking stains. My stomach turned to ice when I saw the long blonde hair hanging over the side of the stretcher.

The librarian let out a gasp and her hands flew to her mouth, "Oh my heavens!" she said, "it's Ms. Bacharach!"

Chapter 8

❖❖❖❖❖❖❖❖❖❖

I gripped the telephone receiver and waited in Mom's office. I couldn't get the picture of Ms. Bacharach on a stretcher out of my head. I squeezed my eyes shut. By the time someone answered the phone, I'd forgotten who I was calling. "Hi, this is Perk Sinclair."

"That's nice, this is Jack Sinclair." Dad's voice startled me.

"Dad! Ms. Bacharach went to the hospital in an ambulance. I need to go there, and Mom can't leave. She said I should call you." I held my breath.

"Slow down, I can barely understand you."

"She's my friend, Dad. If you don't take me I'm going to hitchhike." I was a little surprised at myself, but it felt good to be tough. "I will. I'm not kidding."

Dad chuckled. "The hell you will. I'll meet you in front of the school in twenty minutes. Let me talk to your mother."

"Wow! Thanks, Dad, thanks! Please hurry!" I almost threw the phone at Mom. I could tell she was as surprised as I was that Dad agreed to leave work and pick me up.

The bell had rung but students were still hanging around and talking about Ms. Bacharach. I raced to my locker, slowing down only when a teacher called after me, "No running!" I threw my things in, and paused when I saw the envelope from Loretta. I folded it up and put in into my back pocket.

I imagined a funeral, Ms. Bacharach's funeral. Everyone stared at me because I was been a friend of Ms. Bacharach's. They knew I was sad and they felt badly for me. I shivered. "What am I doing? I shouldn't be thinking that!" I hated myself when I thought these things, but I couldn't help it. They just popped into my head.

Really, I was scared and felt helpless. I couldn't picture someone dying, especially someone I loved.

"Please, God," I whispered. "Let her and the baby be alright."

I got outside just as Dad pulled up in his pickup truck. "Let's go," he growled. He pulled away before I was completely in the car. I used both hands to swing the door shut.

"Why are you mad? I didn't do anything." I stared out the window. Dad didn't answer. "Dad, do you think Ms. Bacharach could die?"

"I have no idea. Your mother knows more about it than I do."

Dad exhaled sharply, ending the conversation. That was fine with me.

He dropped me at the front entrance to the hospital. "You may have to do all your waiting in the lobby since you're underage. I'll go down the street to McCann's and have a beer. Come get me when you've had enough."

I watched the truck pull away. Sometimes he left me feeling hollowed out like a pumpkin.

I turned and looked at the cold brick entryway of the hospital. All of my daydreaming about being the main attraction at a funeral was over. This was the real thing, and I was terrified that my friend and her baby might not make it through the ordeal.

Dad was right about not being allowed into intensive care. The front desk said I had to wait downstairs.

After what seemed like forever, a woman introduced herself as Ms. Bacharach's sister. "The nurse said you were waiting."

I jumped to my feet and looked into the face of a woman who looked like a younger version of Ms. Bacharach. "Hi! Is she okay, I mean is she ...."

"The doctors say she's stable right now. She'd started to hemorrhage. They don't know why. They are going to deliver the baby early." The woman wrung her hands. "I have to tell you, I'm terrified of hospitals. I'm glad you're here. Her husband is in New York City. We just managed to reach him, and it will be hours before he gets here!"

She took my hand and let out a shuddery sigh.

"I don't mean to ramble on but I'm worried about my sister."

"It's okay, you aren't rambling." I was starting to see that I could help her calm down. "Everything will work out."

Ms. Bacharach's sister came out every fifteen minutes or so and kept me updated. It seemed to be a big relief for her to have a reason to leave the intensive care unit.

"They are going to do the Cesarean section now. The doctor says I can stay in there with her. You should go home. Thank you, Perk." She kissed my forehead.

I nodded. I was worried about my teacher but I also felt important. I hadn't thought anyone would actually rely on me for anything, especially an adult.

I stayed at the hospital until a nurse told me Ms. Bacharach delivered a four pound boy, and for the moment everyone was out of the woods.

It was dark and rainy outside. The cold fresh air felt wonderful after being inside for so long. I felt grownup. I spent a moment on the hospital steps, gazing at the lights reflected in the slick street.

I buttoned my sweater, and started for McCann's where Dad said he'd be. I felt a pang of worry when I realized how late it was. He would be irritated.

"Perk, Perk! Over here!" I saw Mom waving from across the street. She had a rain slicker on. Bridey was in the car seat in back.

I was confused. "I'm supposed to meet Dad."

"Just come here! I don't want to scream at you from across the street!"

I waited for a break in traffic, and then sprinted to the car. I had a worried feeling in my stomach.

"Dad got tired of waiting, so Bridey and I came to pick you up." Mom held the car door open.

"He left me? Why didn't he just tell me he wanted to go. He knew where I was." It made me mad that he was acting like I had done something wrong.

"Perk, please don't make a scene. Let's stop at BurgerWorld and get something for dinner. Dad can cool off for a while."

Bridey clapped her hands together and yelled "Cheeseburgers!"

"Mom, was he really mad at me? You know, Ms. Bacharach's husband wasn't even there. Her sister said I was a big help!"

"That's great, Perk." Mom sighed. "I don't know why it's such a mystery to you, Perk. Your father is a little moody. He's always been that way, he probably always will be that way."

"In case you're interested, they delivered the baby early. He's premature."

"Of course I'm interested. Ms. Bacharach is a friend of mine too. We do happen to work together."

Bridey clapped her hands again, and I slunk down in my seat and stared out the window. Maybe I would just never understand my parents.

We pulled up to a big clown face. I ordered two cheeseburgers, fries, and a large vanilla milkshake.

Mom looked at me. "Oh, Perk! That's too much!"

"Well, then take me to Angels Salad Bar and I'll order salad! You picked this place, and I'm hungry!" If Mom wasn't interested in me saving the day for Ms. Bacharach's sister, then what I ate for dinner wasn't any of her business.

I liked fast food places. We always ate in the car so I had plenty of privacy from Mom when I went inside to throw up in the bathroom. I would never, ever dream of eating fast food if I couldn't throw up.

I ate quickly. The worst thing that could happen would be for Mom to finish eating first. Then she might decide to start the car and head for home.

"I'll be right back." I grabbed my bag and ran inside the restaurant.

"Can I have the key for the ladies room please?" I held out my hand to a girl behind the counter.

"It's out of order." The girl didn't seem sorry at all. My mouth dropped open.

"Well, what am I supposed to do?" I asked.

The girl shrugged.

I started feeling panicky. I had to get rid of this food. I looked outside and saw Mom and Bridey in the car. I slipped out and around the rear of the restaurant. It was raining heavily now. I stood in the shadow of a big overflowing dumpster. The darkness was scary but I hoped the stench from the garbage would help me be sick.

I looked around to make sure I was alone and pushed my fingers down my throat. I felt the usual relief at being able to throw up. It made me feel like I was going to be alright.

"Perk! What are you doing!"

My legs threatened to buckle. It was Mom.

"Oh, God! Get back to the car right now!" Mom said angrily and disappeared around the corner.

I stood still for a moment. I couldn't believe Mom had caught me. I wiped off my hands and slowly walked towards the waiting Volvo.

"I don't know what you think you are doing. How long have you been making yourself throw up?" Mom asked.

"I don't know, a while! It keeps me from getting fat. You said you didn't want me to get fat." I could hear my voice shaking.

"I also don't want you to be so stupid. I guess I lose on both counts." Mom started the car, and swore when the engine died. She slammed her hands on the steering wheel and tried the engine again. She shifted into gear and screeched out of the parking lot.

Tears rolled down my cheeks. We drove home without speaking.

Chapter 9

❖❖❖❖❖❖❖❖❖❖❖

I sat on the edge of the bathtub. Mom ordered me to wait there until she had put Bridey to bed. The house was so quiet I was sure I could feel it breathing.

I pulled my shirt up and turned sideways in the bathroom mirror. The fast food dinner was making my stomach stick out. I sighed and sat down again.

I didn't want Mom to yell at me, but I did feel a little relieved. Maybe it was good she had seen me.

I heard Mom's footsteps on the stairs. My heart started racing. She opened and shut the door quietly but I knew it was only because she didn't want to wake up Dad. She was radiating anger. Her hands were shaking and her mouth was a tight white line. I was shocked to see what seemed like hatred in her eyes.

"I cannot figure out, for the life of me, why you choose to make yourself throw up. You don't have a broken home, we don't abuse you. Apparently you're trying to get back at me for something." Mom hissed the words at me.

I worked the corner of a washcloth in my hands. I felt as if I would snap in half.

"Mom, I'm sorry, I thought you didn't want me to get fat! I'm sorry....I love you!" I sobbed and tried to throw myself into her arms.

Mom pushed me back. "Don't think that you can make everything okay by telling me you love me, and please don't make this my fault. I never said 'Gee Perk, you look fat, why not try bulimia!'"

"I want to leave!" I pushed past Mom. "I should just leave if you hate me so much!"

I slammed the bathroom door and ran to my room. I was crying so hard I could barely catch my breath.

"Good! Go! You're a liar anyway, I don't like liars living here!" Mom re-slammed the bathroom door.

Red and blue lights flashed and popped at the corners of my eyes. I wanted to scream. Larry tried to squeeze himself under my bed. I slammed my bedroom door.

I heard the bathroom door fly open.

"Don't you dare! Don't you dare slam a door in this house, Priscilla!" Mom screamed through my locked door.

"What the hell is going on around here!" Dad yelled.

I kicked my bed, hard. The pain in my foot infuriated me. "I hate you! I hate you!"

"Go to bed." I heard Dad say firmly to Mom. I had never heard Dad use that tone of voice with her. "Right now, go to bed."

"You don't know what she's doing, Jack. I can't take it anymore," my mother said to Dad. She sounded like she was sobbing.

The floorboards creaked outside of their bedroom and I heard the door shut. I sat for a few minutes in complete silence, straining to hear what was happening over the sound of my breathing. The house was silent, like nothing had ever happened.

Mom acted like I was doing this on purpose, to hurt her. I should have realized that she'd take this personally. After all, she was a children's counselor. Wouldn't a daughter with an eating disorder make her a failure?

I looked around my room. There was no way I would be falling asleep anytime soon. I saw the envelope from Loretta lying on the floor underneath my backpack and jacket. I stuffed the envelope into my full wastebasket. I watched as it slowly unfolded itself and fell back onto the floor. I kicked it and then picked it up. "Maybe it will bore me to sleep, right Larry?" Larry looked at me as if he would rather be left out of it.

I tore open the top and dumped the contents on my bed. There were several xeroxed articles on eating disorders and a sheet of phone numbers. They were fastened with a paper clip to a Polaroid picture and a handwritten note.

Written in smudgy ink on the bottom of the photo it said "Loretta Gauthier." It was a girl in a hospital bed with tubes in her nose and arms. She looked like a skeleton, and her eyes looked lifeless and flat. I stared at the photo for a long time because it didn't look anything like Loretta to me. I opened the note. It said:

Perk,

I'm glad you are reading this. I thought this photo of me might get your attention. Before I got married, I was anorexic. Later, after I was "cured" I became bulimic. I almost died from both diseases, and they ruined my life at the time. If this sounds familiar or interesting to you, please call me and we can talk.

Loretta

"I don't look like that! Why did she give me that stupid photo?" I asked Larry. He pretended to be asleep. I decided that everyone was just going to have to leave me alone, and that was that.

I could tell Mom it was all a misunderstanding. Everything would be okay, I would make it that way.

I tossed and turned for most of the night. I couldn't shut my head off. I tried to think of ways to make Mom see I was trying to be a better daughter. When I finally dropped off at dawn I dreamed about the little demon girl again.

The girl tried to kiss me. I wanted to run, but I felt as if I were drugged. My arms and legs were like lead. The demon child grabbed my arm, and I could smell her yellow skin and hair. With a ragged fingernail, she scratched a word in the skin of my wrist. I knew the message was terribly urgent, but I couldn't quite make out what it said.

Chapter 10

❖❖❖❖❖❖❖❖❖❖❖❖❖

When I woke up Larry was whimpering in his sleep. I reached out and tickled his chest, setting his back feet in motion. I smiled, until I remembered last night.

I tried to step out of bed without making the floorboards creak while I slipped into my bathrobe.

"C'mon Larry," I whispered and wrapped the fur of the scruff of his neck in my fingers. I let him lead the way downstairs.

Mom was cutting tomatoes on a wooden board. The knife sliced through the fruit and hit the board with a loud 'CHOP' that made me jump.

"I don't know why they have to put a label on every single stupid tomato. I don't have time to peel little labels off all over the place!" Mom picked up a piece of tomato and tried to remove a small slice of sticky paper.

"Yeah, it's pretty stupid." I wasn't sure what else to say.

She gave me an irritated look and threw the unwanted pieces into the sink. "Here's what we're going to do, starting immediately. You're going to keep a diary of everything you eat, every day, and show it to me at the end of the day."

"Mom, I'm not going to throw up any more. I promise. You don't have to worry."

"I'm having a hard time with this, Perk. I am under so much pressure at work. This is just one more thing to deal with."

"That's what I'm saying, Mom. I'll stop. Everything is okay." It seemed pretty easy to me.

"I'd like to believe that, but you make it difficult." Mom pushed her hair off her forehead. "You disappoint me, Perk. Again and again I expect you to do better and you don't. I can't live your life for you."

I looked at Mom, and realized that I wasn't paying attention. I hated this speech. It made me feel stupid. It was easier to just veg-out.

"Do you have any idea what I was talking about?" Mom asked.

"Of course I do!" I said. "I'm not an idiot!"

"I'm going to take a shower and get Bridey up. We can continue this conversation later." Mom sighed and took her coffee upstairs.

"No problem," I mumbled. I shuffled over to the kitchen table and draped myself across it.

I didn't have the energy to get dressed. I decided

to break my no-breakfast rule. I looked in the pantry and was delighted when I saw a full box of my favorite water crackers. Nice and light. A bag of chocolate morsels grabbed my eye.

I knew I shouldn't, but all of a sudden I really wanted them. I reached into the bottom drawer of the pantry and pulled out a paper bag. I crammed the chocolate morsels, the crackers, and a new box of cookies into the bag. I saw a can of wild blueberries in heavy syrup, shrugged, and tossed it into the collection. I was beginning to feel unfocused.

I felt a light spidery feeling tickle my neck. I batted around at the back of my head with my hand. Again, a slight touch... I turned around, half expecting to see Mom standing there, but I was alone. My heart beat faster. The feeling was still there, as if someone were breathing right behind me, touching my hair very gently. I remembered the demon girl.

"Mom!" I yelled. My voice sounded weird in the empty kitchen. I was afraid to call out again.

I heard something and froze. It sounded like a radio playing with the volume turned way down. It was the voices again, whispering, whispering.

The phone rang. I jumped and screamed. Mom walked into the kitchen, struggling to fasten an earring. I hid the bag under my bathrobe.

"Perk, what is the matter? What are you screaming about!" She answered the phone.

I ran upstairs to my room and shut the door. The voices and the prickly feeling at the back of my neck had stopped, but I still felt weird. I wondered what Mom would think if she knew I was going crazy. My mouth pulled down and I wanted to cry. Instead, I reached into the bag and opened the box of cookies. I shoved one into my mouth. The melty chocolate and crunchy cookie made me feel instantly better. I jammed another one in.

"Perk!" Mom called from the bottom of the stairs.

I jumped again and wiped the cookie crumbs from my face with my pillow. I groaned when I saw the smear of chocolate across the pillowcase. I flipped the pillow over just as Mom walked through the door.

"That was Marilyn. She's running late. I need to get to work right now. Can you please watch Bridey until Marilyn gets here? Then you can ride your bike. I'll tell the attendance office you'll be late."

I nodded yes. I had cookies in my teeth.

Mom looked hard at me. I tried to meet her eyes but it was impossible. I studied my feet. I had an awful feeling there were cookie crumbs on my face.

"I have to go." Mom turned and walked downstairs.

I brought Bridey into my room and gave her a photo album to look at. I tried to find something to wear and ended up changing my clothes three times. I wished I hadn't eaten those cookies. Bridey put a pair of my underwear on over her pajamas.

"C'mon, silly! Those are mine." I picked her up. "Let's go downstairs." I saw the cookies sticking out from under my blanket and reached for them. I shoved another one in my mouth.

"Cookie!" squealed Bridey, clapping her hands.

"Okay, just one." I gave us each one. "Let's take these and have a cookie picnic for breakfast."

I looked at the clock, trying to figure out how much time I had until Marilyn got here. I was going to have to throw up. There was just no way I could eat half a box of cookies and then leave the house.

I poured cereal for both of us, and sprinkled several spoonfuls of sugar on mine. I finished mine quickly and poured another bowl. Then I made toast, with lots of butter and honey.

I took Bridey's cereal away before she was done eating, and ate it on the way to the sink. I needed to figure out what to do with her while I threw up.

I decided to take her outside with me before Marilyn arrived.

"C'mon Honey Bunny, let's go outside!" I said. I grabbed Bridey's red sweater and pulled it on over her stubby little arms.

"Outside!" Bridey grinned and ran for the door. I smiled as I noticed her toddler legs didn't quite bend when she ran.

I stuffed paper towels and some gum in my pocket. I held Bridey's hand and we galloped sideways down the steep hill. Larry ran to catch up, barking with excitement.

"Isn't it pretty, Bridey?" I pointed at the curled, green buds on the trees. The lawn was wet, and the Esopus sparkled in the morning sun. The air felt cool and fresh from the creek.

"Yah!" Bridey nodded enthusiastically.

"Bridey, I have to go over here for a minute. Play with Larry, okay?"

Bridey looked at me, and then shrieked in glee, boxing Larry on his ears. I could hardly concentrate. I was feeling that spidery feeling on my neck again, and hearing the wispy voices.

"I'll be right back." I ran to the edge of the woods, and ducked behind a bush. I looked around to make sure no one could see me. If I turned my head to the left I had a perfect view of Bridey through the hemlock.

I tried to make myself throw up, but I was too tense. I told myself to ignore the panicky feeling and take a deep breath. Bridey was holding on tight to Larry's tail. She giggled and screamed in delight as he pulled her around the lawn.

I still wasn't able to throw up. I could try using a spoon but I hadn't brought one with me. I looked at the house. I was running out of time. If I ran really fast, I could get the spoon and get back down here before Bridey even knew I was gone.

I decided to take the chance. I ran across the lawn and up the hill. I slipped and fell on one knee. "Damn!" Larry came running to my rescue. "Larry, get back down there with Bridey!"

"Perkie!" Bridey called. "I want to come with you!" She ran towards me.

"No no, Honey, I'll be right back! I promise!" I was ten feet away from the house, too close not to go. I ran inside, groaning when I saw my muddy footprints on the clean linoleum floor. I ran to the utensil drawer and grabbed a spoon.

"Okay, okay, okay," I sing-songed, did a quick turn-around and headed back to the door. Yes! I made it.

It took a second to register that something was wrong. Larry was barking at the water. Bridey had vanished.

"Bridey? Bridey! Oh my God!" I felt as if I was running in dream quicksand. I couldn't hear anything over the noise of the water. I stopped breathing and ran as fast as I could towards the smudge of red sweater just under the surface.

"Move goddamnit! Move!" I shoved Larry out of the way and leapt into the icy water. It was so cold it took my breath away. I saw Bridey's hair and grabbed for it, bringing us both to the surface of the water. Larry was still barking.

My heart pounded in my ears. I struggled to push Bridey up onto the bank, and heaved myself out of the water. Everything was moving much too slowly.

"What happened!" Marilyn screamed as she skidded down the hill and fell on her rear end in the grass. "Perk! What happened!"

I flipped over my little sister so she lay on her stomach. She was limp and cold.

"I killed her! Oh my God, I killed my little sister!"

Chapter 11

❖❖❖❖❖❖❖❖❖❖❖

I sat on a hospital gurney, and chewed on a strand of my hair. It tasted like the Esopus. I was chilled to the bone and shivering. They had taken off my wet clothes and wrapped me in scratchy blankets. No one would tell me what had happened to Bridey.

Mom and Dad hadn't said a word to me since they arrived at the hospital. I knew they were here because a nurse had told me. That was over an hour ago. I didn't blame them. There was no doubt in my mind now that they would hate me. I knew I thoroughly deserved it.

A doctor stopped to give me an exam in the hallway. He poked and prodded and wrote things down. He didn't bother to talk to me. I was sure everyone here knew what I had done.

"Do you know anything about my sister? Her name is Bridey Sinclair," I asked.

"No, I don't. I'm sorry." The doctor impatiently waved a flashlight and tongue depressor around trying to gain access to my throat. "Open up, please." His eyebrows arched up like he saw something interesting. He paused to look at my face for the first time, and then went back to my throat.

"You have quite a few unusual blisters. Do you have any idea why?" the doctor asked, frowning.

"No." Blisters were the least of my problems right now.

"Do you throw up?" he asked.

"No!" I said a little too loudly, but he had caught me off guard.

The doctor felt my throat again, and made a note on his clipboard. "I don't see any signs of hypothermia, but I'm going to suggest you stay tonight anyway, just to be safe."

"Whatever," I mumbled to his disappearing back.

The swinging doors slammed open, and Dad burst in. He charged up to me, grabbed both sides of the blankets and pulled me off the gurney. I sprawled to the ground in a heap, and scrambled to keep my hospital gown shut.

"You were supposed to watch her! How could you be so goddamned stupid! I don't even want to look at you." He spoke in a low voice and his eyes glittered with anger. I saw Mom standing behind him. Her face was hard to read. I wanted some privacy. I was embarrassed.

All of a sudden, I remembered wishing that I had time to finish throwing up when I realized Bridey was gone. I pressed my fists into my eyes and screamed, "Shut up!" in my head. I should die, not Bridey!

"Get your crazy hands off that child or I'll call the police!" A heavy set, black nurse manhandled Dad away from me.

"She's my daughter, damnit!" he growled.

"I don't care if she's Princess Diana! You won't be beating children on my shift or in my hospital!" The nurse put her hands on her hips and thrust her chin out, as if to dare him to test her.

Dad put an unlit cigarette in his mouth and glared at me, as well as everyone else in the corridor. He ran a hand through his hair and walked down the hall to the elevator.

"I'll be right there," Mom called after him, and then she watched me again. I could tell she had something to say. I wanted her to yell at me.

I stared at the floor. The nurse didn't know what I had done, otherwise she would have understood why he wanted to hurt me. "He doesn't usually do that," I said to the nurse.

"Well, I should hope not," the nurse said. "Let me help you back up on the table."

Mom walked up to me, "I'll do it." She waited until the nurse was out of earshot. Her tone was cool. "They said I should admit you tonight, so I'll see you tomorrow." She rubbed her forehead. "Honestly, I don't know if you can come home right now, not if you are going to endanger our family."

"Okay." I felt tears streaming down my face. "Mom, is Bridey....?" Sobs choked me, and squeezed my heart.

"She's okay. They're going to keep her for a few days, and do some tests. If it was still Winter and Marilyn had not shown up, she would be dead. That's all I have to say."

I felt my body sag as if someone had hit me. I cried even harder. That was all I needed to hear, that Bridey was alive. I could worry about where I was going to live later.

Mom wouldn't look at me before she left. I felt momentary panic replace my tears. I had never stayed overnight in a hospital before.

"Shut up. You deserve to be scared," I said softly to myself.

The nurse who had spoken up for me brought me a robe and put it over my shoulders. "C'mon, Honey. We'll go to your room. Blow your nose. I'm sure your parents are scared to death. People sometimes say things they don't mean when they are upset."

I stayed quiet. I knew I was bad. Nothing anyone could say would make that change. "Can I see my sister?"

"Not now, she needs to rest. So do you."

"How about the maternity ward? Can I go there?"

"Oh, are you planning on having a baby?" The

nurse asked and chuckled.

"No...I mean, I have a friend there." I smiled at the nurse. I liked her.

"We'll go in a little while. First, I'd like to talk to you now that we're alone."

"I swear, Dad's never done that before. He was just angry."

"I'm glad to hear it, but that's not what I wanted to ask. The doctor who examined you said you have symptoms of bulimia. Do you know what that is?" The nurse watched my eyes.

My heart sped up. I didn't think the doctor was going to make a big deal about it. Suddenly I connected throwing up to the blisters the doctor saw. It scared me to think that throwing up had filled my throat with blisters.

"Yeah, but I had a flu. I threw up a lot, I get sick all the time." I had an urge to run. The room was out of focus behind the nurse.

"Save your breath, Dearie. I see this all the time. I can introduce you to a woman upstairs who ruptured her stomach from eating and throwing up. We had a girl last month who starved to death right under our noses. We had to feed her through an I.V., and she kept ripping out the tubes and telling us to stop because she was getting fat. Well, she's not getting fat anymore." The nurse sat on the bed with me. "Make no mistake, whether you are starving yourself or throwing up you have a very serious illness."

I could barely understand what the nurse was saying. I just wanted her to stop talking. "I'll be fine," I said.

"Maybe you will and maybe you won't. Our girl on the I.V. kept saying that, too."

Chapter 12

❖❖❖❖❖❖❖❖❖❖❖❖❖

I was awake all night thinking about Bridey, and that I was spending the night in a hospital. My life just seemed to have crashed and burned, and I wasn't completely sure how or why.

I lay in bed and gazed into the hallway. I thought about calling Evvie, but knew there was really no point. Besides, I didn't think I could gather the energy to pick up the phone. Every muscle in my body felt useless. I rolled over on my side and wrapped my arms around my stomach. I stretched my legs, trying to get rid of the shame, guilt and disappointment that filled my body. It didn't work.

I had always secretly pictured myself a role-model, honest, a good friend, a good sister. Things hadn't worked out that way. I hated to think that I had failed. I didn't want to be the "The Girl who Throws Up" at school. When Dom found out, he would be completely grossed out. So would Evvie. So would everybody. I was exhausted. I was so tired of myself.

I could remember clearly the first time I had thrown up. It seemed to be the perfect way to control my body, the same body that had caused me so much grief for my entire life. I sighed and turned over.

"Are you asleep, honey?" The nurse gently shook my shoulder. "We can find your friend in maternity now if you'd like. Your mother will be back this afternoon. Life is moving on, so let's get you out of bed."

I rolled over and looked at the nurse. "Okay." I was going to cry. My chin was quivering. I sat up and folded my hands tightly in my lap. I kept my head lowered as I cried, so the nurse wouldn't see. Hot tears splashed on my hands.

"There, Honey, you're too young to be carrying all that around. Maybe something is telling you that it's time to do something different, like get well. Throwing up seems like an awful mean thing to do to yourself."

"I don't want to get fat!" I wailed.

"I didn't either, but look at my behind! I'm not willing to die over it." She sat on the bed. "See, you gotta figure out how to fill that emptiness in your heart with love and healthy things, not cookies and ice cream."

"So what am I supposed to do?" I kept hearing that I had a problem, but I had no idea how to fix it.

"It takes time and work. Just relax for now. First, let's go see your friend."

❖

Ms. Bacharach was sitting up in bed and waiting for me. "Perk, I can't believe you're here!"

I ran to the bed and hugged my teacher. "Where's the baby? I want to see him!"

Ms. Bacharach pulled me close. "You will. First tell me what's going on." She squeezed my shoulders.

I started crying again. It seemed the tears just wouldn't stop. I told her everything, about the bulimia, about my sister, and my parents, even about Loretta Gauthier. Ms. Bacharach just listened until I was done.

"Perk, I'm sorry. I knew something was wrong, I guess I thought you'd tell me when you were ready. Don't worry about anything, just concentrate on getting well." Ms. Bacharach looked excited. "I'll help you, and you should talk to Loretta. She offered, what could be better?"

I shook my head. "What about Mom and Dad?"

"What about them? If you were my daughter, I would do everything I could to help you. If things don't work out, Perk, then you can stay with us. I mean it! We're going to need help with the baby. I'll check with my husband, but I'm sure he won't mind. You can also help keep my studio clean. You could be my apprentice!"

I looked at my teacher. This all sounded like a dream.

"It's time for you to see my little boy. We named him John Henry. It sounded like a strong name for a strong child. He's fighting the good fight, that's for sure." Ms. Bacharach's eyes became shiny, and she looked directly at me. "I guess he knows it's worth the effort."

I followed the maternity nurse down the darkened hallway. It felt quiet and comfortable here. An orderly wheeled a woman with her new baby towards the elevator. The father hovered protectively over the wheelchair. The couple looked terrified, as if the baby might fly out of their arms at any second. The nurse looked at me and smiled.

"Amateurs," she chuckled. "Here we go, the Bacharach baby is in the front row. We've had to intubate him, his lungs are premature. The poor little guy has been touch and go from the start."

I was startled. This wasn't like any baby I had ever seen. He had tubes in his nose, and a clear plastic hood over his head. I had never seen a creature so fragile, and tiny. His little fists were clenched. A nurse reached in through the sides of the incubator and adjusted his tubes. Her hands were in protective gloves.

Now I understood what Ms. Bacharach meant by

fighting the good fight. I just didn't have a clue how to do that for myself. I felt like I had been lying to myself and everyone else, and now here I was at the hospital.

I thought about the picture of Loretta Gauthier when she was sick. It reminded me of the baby, emaciated, the tubes, the hospital, and the threat of death.

"Oh..." I sighed and leaned my forehead on the glass. I wiped the steam from my breath off with my sleeve. This little baby who was fighting for his life didn't have a choice. He would probably trade his predicament with mine in a second. Still, I felt helpless.

I wanted to scream all of a sudden. Everybody kept telling me they would help me but they didn't seem to understand. If I gained even one pound...I just wouldn't be able to do it! Once I started eating I didn't know how to stop. It was like something else took over. I felt my stomach harden into a tight little knot. Anger crept up the back of my neck and into my shoulder blades.

I wondered what it was that everyone wanted from me. I balled my fists and walked quickly down the hall. I wanted to hit something and make it hurt as much as I did. My chest heaved.

"How dare Mom tell me I might have to move out! She just better figure out a way to deal with me! She just better!"

I kicked a door marked exit and cried out in pain when it didn't open. Enraged, I pushed the door hard and found myself in the stairway.

"This isn't fair! I'm all alone! She should help me! Dad should help me!" I yelled at the top of my lungs. "I can't do this by myself. I hurt! I hurt all over! I'm really, really afraid." Doubling over and holding my stomach, sorrow and pain filled and overwhelmed me. I slid down the wall and sat on the ground, shaking. I started crying and felt the pain start coming out. "I'm so afraid...." I moaned in a little voice. "Please help me...." It felt good to say that. It felt surprisingly good.

"What in God's name is happening in here?" An old security guard ran through the heavy door and stared at me. He looked worried and had one hand on his security club.

I didn't know what to say. I wanted to tell the guard I felt better, but it didn't seem appropriate. I stood up and brushed off my clothes. "I'm okay."

"Well, that's good because you're not supposed to be hollerin' in the stairwell. I'll call a nurse for you. Where's your room?"

"Downstairs, I'll go now." I seemed to have one voice in my head at the moment instead of ten. I got to my feet and felt a little lighter, and clearer.

"I'll take a little walk with you, Miss. I want to make sure you get there." He looked at me sideways and gestured towards the stairwell door with a nod of his head.

I found my favorite nurse when I got back to my floor. "There you are! My shift is done, but I'd like to do something before I go." She walked me to my room.

I jumped up on my bed and let my legs dangle off the side. "I wish you weren't going."

"I spend quite enough hours here, thank you very much. We need to call your folks and tell them you're ready for treatment so we can get you into a support group before you leave today. The doctor should take a look at you to see what kind of shape you're in. Bulimics are prone to heart trouble among many other unpleasant things."

My skin goosebumped. "Tell them now? I-I-I don't know if I'm ready! What if they don't want me to do this?"

"They may not. Don't assume that, though. You should find a support group too. We'll help you do all of that. How about we call your folks now?"

I was so nervous I almost felt like laughing. I held my pillow over my face and screamed in exasperation. I knew now was the time for me to be brave and try and help myself. "I wish I didn't have to do this. It's not fair."

"Yeah, and it's not fair I gotta work for a living when my true destiny is to be rich and famous."

"Okay! Call! Call!" I flopped back on my bed and threw the pillow at the wall. I knew the nurse was not going to stop bothering me. I wanted to rely on that. It made me feel good.

"Good girl!" She patted my arm and laughed. "I'll be right back, and we'll get to it." She winked at me.

I watched the nurse leave the room and bit the skin around my fingernails. Now I was feeling hungry, starved in fact. I felt like I was waiting to be brought to a firing squad. Even though I was scared, I was a little proud of myself for letting the nurse call my parents. I felt courageous.

I stared at the phone on the table beside the bed. My heart was thumping and my teeth were clenched. I thought about calling home before the nurse came back. I'd tell Mom and Dad it was all lies. I didn't need help, or tests. Nothing was wrong with me.

But I didn't. I stayed on the bed and kept swinging my legs and biting my fingernails.

I decided I would wait and see.

Chapter 13

❖❖❖❖❖❖❖❖❖❖❖❖

I sat with the nurse while she called my parents. It sounded like she kept getting interrupted. That didn't surprise me.

"No, I was not aware you were a child psychologist, Mrs. Sinclair. Yes, of course the whole thing is troubling, but we do need to think of Perk."

The nurse looked at me and smiled while she listened. I shook my head at her. I could tell it wasn't going well.

"No, you're right, I'm not a doctor. I am authorized to inform you of the situation, however. Perk is anxious to get better." She gave me a thumbs up sign.

"Mrs. Sinclair, we have an eating disorders support group that meets here every morning. I highly recommend Perk sit in on one before she goes home today. Support groups are a very effective part of the recovery process." She listened for another moment.

"Oh, we've got a code red here! I've gotta jump off, Mrs. Sinclair. Thanks for your time." She hung up the phone and rolled her chair close to me.

"What's a code red?" I asked.

"A code red is when you have got to get off the phone!" She said, laughing. "It sounds to me like your mother is having a little trouble digesting all of this. It's going to make your job harder."

My heart sank. "What's my job?" I asked. This all seemed too big for me, especially now that I knew Mom was still mad.

"To get well, Perk. That's it for right now. You try and get through a day, minute by minute, without doing any harm to your body. And don't throw up, no matter what. Not even if your butt falls off."

"Okay," I said, and laughed.

She took my hand. Hers felt warm and dry. "I like you, Perk. You're a strong girl. I want you to be one of the ones who make it."

My mouth pulled down, and my throat tightened up. "I'm really, really scared." I started crying, and she hugged me.

"Of course you are. That's completely natural, Honey." She squeezed me tight. "Now, you got a group to get to. If you can't find a ride to the hospital to attend this one, then you need to find one or start one close to you, okay? I'll leave pamphlets with phone numbers with the day nurse. Rely on the people that have offered to help, like your friend with the baby upstairs. Promise, girl?"

"I wish you would stay."

"I already told you! I got to get outta here! You can always get me at the hospital. As long as you're trying to get well, I'll help." She handed me a slip of paper with the room number of the group on it.

"Are all of these people going to be weird?" I asked.

"Weird as you, Honey. Get going." She winked and gave me her thumbs up signal again. "Oh, your mother was here all night with your sister. Did you know she was in your room for a while?"

"She was? I didn't think I ever fell asleep!"

"Well, I guess you did, 'cause she was here." She smiled and walked down the hall.

I was confused. I had been pretty sure it was going to be bad with Mom and Dad, really bad. Maybe Mom still loved me if she came to visit me, or maybe she was just trying to decide what to do.

I got to the conference room where my group was. I took a deep breath and went right to a table that had bottles of juice and ice. I didn't want to look around. I didn't want to meet anyone. Sunlight streamed in the windows and made me feel too hot. I loaded a cup with ice and checked the label of the juice. I hated drinking juice because it had so many calories.

"I know what you're thinking," a voice behind me said.

I turned and saw a guy with shoulder length blonde hair. He looked right into my eyes and smiled.

"You think it's too fattening. It's true, I guess, juice does have a lot of sugar." He poured a cup for himself. "I'll share," he said, offering me the bottle.

"No, that's okay. I'm not thirsty." I was, but I wanted a diet soda.

"My name is Jason. My sister is a bulimic. She was a patient here and came to one group. She's still throwing up. I come so I can fill her in on stuff."

"That's nice of you." I sucked a piece of ice. I couldn't believe this guy was talking to me.

"I guess. But the counselors say I need to find my own support group, for family members. They say my sister needs to be responsible for her own recovery. She won't do it though."

"My name is Perk. I still think it's really nice of you. It means you love her." I followed him to a semi-circle of chairs. "Is it okay if I sit by you? I mean, are there assigned seats or anything?"

"No, sit. I know I'm not supposed to say this, but you shouldn't worry about your weight. You look good to me. I think you're really pretty."

I felt my face turn completely red, and I'm sure he could tell because he smiled at me. So far, several people today had told me they liked me and wanted me to get better. One of them was a guy, an amazingly cute guy. I felt full all of a sudden, and I just wanted to leave the group and run around and sing.

"Leslie, this is Perk," Jason introduced me to a girl

who looked like a skeleton. She rolled an I.V. pole to a chair and fell into the seat. She seemed exhausted. Her thin hair was wound tightly into a ballerina bun. She gave me a half wave and closed her eyes when she sat down. "That's Janice, and Michael, and April, and Peggy."

It was hard not to stare at Leslie. It didn't seem like she was alive anymore, except when I saw her occasionally jerk herself upright, like she was falling asleep. Everyone else looked like they were teenagers, like me, except Peggy, who seemed pretty old. Her teeth were all rotted.

Peggy threw her pocketbook on the floor. "Can we get some sort of beverage around here besides juice, for heaven's sake? If I can't smoke, I should at least be able to drink what I like, or maybe I don't pay you people enough money!" She turned sideways in her chair and glared angrily out the window. She made me nervous. It felt strange to be in a group with people like her and Leslie.

"Peggy's always mad," Jason whispered. "But she keeps coming to group. She doesn't want to throw up anymore."

The counselor came in and introduced herself. She looked nice. She asked everyone to say their names and "check in." We were supposed to tell her how we were feeling. By the time she got to me I was shaking.

"Can you tell us who you are and how you're doing?" She asked.

"My name is Perk, but I thought I could watch because it's my first time." My face was burning again. I wanted her to stop talking to me.

"Welcome, Perk. How about you tell us what's going on right now." She smiled. "You're in a safe place."

"I'm scared." I got mad because my chin started get all weird again, and I started to cry. I felt like a jerk crying in front of Jason and other people I didn't know. "I don't really want to talk right now."

"We'll go slow," the counselor assured. "You will need to participate soon. Everyone here will be sharing things that are scary to them. Hopefully we'll be able to leave them here so we don't have to eat over them later."

Jason took my hand and squeezed it. I could easily fall in love with him, I thought to myself. I tried to picture Dom in my head. He seemed fuzzy and far away. I squeezed back.

When the group was over, the counselor took my number so she could find me a support group and a therapist in Phoenicia. She put her arm around my shoulder and gave me a hug.

"I'm sorry I started to cry, I can't seem to stop these days," I said. I was embarrassed.

"Don't apologize for crying, Perk! You did a good job. It's hard to talk, but it gets easier. I hope we see you again," she said.

Jason asked if it would be okay if he called me.

"I would really like that." I said.

"Me too," Jason smiled. "I hope you get better fast."

I smiled back.

❖

I wasn't sure if I was allowed to see Bridey. I was afraid to ask. I thought the nurses might tell me she was off limits, since I had almost killed her. But I needed to see my little sister. I figured it might also be my last chance if Mom wanted me to move out.

I had a little time before my physical. I went back to the children's ward and peeked in the rooms as I walked down the hall.

"What are you looking for?" a big nurse carrying a stack of children's books asked.

"Um, Bridey Sinclair," I stammered.

The nurse jerked her head to the left. "209, right there." She padded off down the hall with her books.

My heart started beating fast. I hoped Bridey looked the same, that she didn't have any tubes like Ms. Bacharach's baby. I hoped I hadn't ruined her.

I stuck my head around the big heavy door. There were four cribs. Bridey was sitting up in one of them trying to twist the top off a rattle. The sun lit up her hair. Her forehead was creased in concentration.

"Bridey," I whispered.

"Perkie!" She shrieked, and jumped up. "Perkie, I want out!" She held on to the rim of the crib and started jumping up and down.

"Bridey!" I ran to her, and buried my face in the warm spot between her head and her shoulder. She smelled so good.

"I want up!" Bridey locked her fat little arms around my neck.

"Honey Bunny, I can't yet. I'll get in trouble." I held her pink face in my hands. She looked the same except for dark violet smudges underneath her eyes.

"Bridey, I love you," I said. "I'm a bad sister. I was bad to you, and I'm so, so, sorry. I'm going to do a lot better, and I'll never let you get hurt again," I tried not to start crying. I didn't want to scare her.

Bridey looked at me with big eyes. She put her moist little hands on my face and squeezed my cheeks, hard. "Awwwww." She made a sad face. "Me too."

"Ouch!" I laughed, and hugged her again.

Bridey pulled away and went back to her rattle.

"Mom's going to get us soon, Honey. I'll see you then, okay?" Bridey nodded her head. "I mean what I say, Bridey. I'll do better. I never meant to hurt you."

Bridey looked at me and smiled.

There was a new nurse on duty when I got back after my physical. I knew I wasn't going to like her as much as my nurse. She had drawn-on eyebrows, and she talked too loud.

"Here is a list of phone contacts for you, and your parents. They need to set up an appointment with the therapist as soon as possible," she yelled. She had been handing me papers for the last three minutes. They kept sliding out of my hands.

"What if they don't?" I asked.

She peered at me over her glasses. "Then you make sure that you set up the appointment. Someone will call next week with the results of your physical, unless they find something serious. Then we will contact you sooner."

"What do you mean, like if I've got cancer or something?" I suspected I might. The doctor kept making faces when he was examining me.

"We're not looking for cancer. We're looking for electrolyte imbalance, compromised heart tissue, a ruptured stomach, although you wouldn't be walking around with that, would you," the nurse snapped, handing me another form.

"I guess not. That's all pretty serious, isn't it?" This nurse was making me worry.

"You're in a hospital. I would take the entire situation seriously." The phone rang. "You can wait in your room. Your parents will be here soon." She punched a line on the phone with a fire engine red fingernail, and then cupped the mouthpiece. "Wait, I have something else for you," she hollered, even though I was still standing next to her desk. She handed me a piece of paper. "She came while you were in group."

I unfolded it and smiled when I saw Ms. Bacharach's signature. It read:

Dear Perk,

I was proud when the nurse said you were in group, good for you! John Henry will be here a few weeks, but they're sending me home. You have a bed waiting if you need it. I'll put you right to work. We all want to help you.

Love,
Lauren Bacharach

My eyes clouded up. I went back to my room to pack my stuff, which took about twenty seconds. I looked out the window and thought about everything that had happened today. Everyone wanted me to get well. Everyone was willing to help. I felt older, like the night I had helped Ms. Bacharach's sister. And, I hadn't thrown up since Bridey fell into the creek. That was almost two whole days ago. It seemed like forever.

I thought about Bridey. I guess it wasn't surprising that she would forgive me. She was still a baby, after all. But it meant everything. As long as I kept my promise to her, maybe I could forgive myself.

I couldn't remember ever having so many good things happen to me in one morning. It almost made me stop worrying about Mom and Dad.

Almost.

Chapter 14

❖❖❖❖❖❖❖❖❖❖❖❖❖

Mom was angry, I could tell that a mile away. She smiled at the nurses when they discharged Bridey and me, but her eyes were mad.

"Where's Dad?" I asked when we got in the car. I climbed into the back seat with Bridey.

"He couldn't come." Her voice was tight.

"I'm sorry, Mom. I didn't mean for any of this to happen. I'm going to take care of everything." I rolled down the window and took a deep breath.

She pulled a crumpled tissue out of her pocket and wiped her eyes. "I don't know what I can do for you. I've obviously failed, or you want the whole world to think I did."

"Mom, you didn't. I don't." I wished she wouldn't say that. It made me feel terrible.

"I can't help but feel like you're trying to embarrass me."

Something flashed in me like a breaking dam. "What are you talking about? This is happening to me, not to you! I don't want to throw up! It makes me really sick!" I took a seat belt and flung it against the door. "I was in the hospital!"

"You were in the hospital because you almost let your sister drown! Don't you forget that! You almost killed her! Don't you ever, ever, compare what happened to her to what's happened to you!" She pulled the car to the side of road and slammed the steering wheel with her hands. Bridey started crying. "It's just laziness!"

"Don't you think I feel horrible about what happened to Bridey? I wish I could just erase that whole day but I can't, and you and Dad are going to hate me forever!" I felt like my chest was going to explode. I was so angry and upset I didn't think I would ever feel better.

"Hate you? How could we possibly hate you, Perk! You have no idea how frightened I am. I don't know how to reach you! I love you, Perk, do you hear me?" She turned to me and grabbed my sweater. "Why don't you hear me!"

I pushed her hand away. Bridey started wailing again. "Because all you do is yell, Mom. Nothing is ever good enough for you. I don't know who you think I'm supposed to be!"

"You're my daughter, and you can do better! You just can, period!"

I started crying with Bridey. "You're all wrong,

Mom. I'm doing the very best I can right now, and you don't have a clue. I'm going to leave when we get home, I'll pack my things. Ms. Bacharach said I could come work for her. She said I can stay at her house." I took a deep breath and decided to stop crying. I shivered for a second.

Mom looked at me. "What are you talking about? You're not going anywhere!"

"Yes I am. Admit it, nothing is good with us. You and Dad would rather I just wasn't around, so I'll go. It's all arranged, all I need to do is call her." I slunk down in my seat. Suddenly, I felt calm and grownup. This seemed like the only solution. Bridey was still whimpering.

Mom started the car. She didn't say a word. Neither did I.

She pulled off of Route 28, drove down to the water, and parked. We sat in silence for a minute. I stared out the window.

"Perk, it never occurred to me that you would leave. I don't want you to. I shouldn't have said any of the things I said. I just feel helpless." She got out of her seat and squeezed in the back with me.

"The counselor told me I need to focus on myself." I didn't look at Mom. "I can't do that if you guys are going to be mad at me all the time."

"Your counselor is right, Honey. Please don't go to Ms. Bacharach's yet. I really do want all of us to be a family again." Mom put her arm around me. I felt hot tears and squeezed my eyes shut.

"What am I going to do about Dad?" I asked.

"I'll explain things to him. Both of us feel like we've failed you. It's not fair, but it's easier to feel angry at you about that than look at how ashamed we are."

I didn't know what to say.

"Can I give you a hug?" Mom took me in her arms, and when I tried to pull away she held on to me for a long time. It felt good to hold my mother, and have her hold me back. I felt all the anger in my chest dissolve.

We didn't say anything else on the way home. Bridey was mad at us for ignoring her. She kept throwing her toys out of her car seat and yelling at me to pick them up.

When we got home, Dad was working outside on his truck. A couple of empty beer bottles sat next to his toolbox in the grass.

Larry jumped up and put both feet on my chest.

"Larry bear!" I kissed him right on his nose and wiped the wetness off with my sleeve. "Ewww, doggie! You slimed me." I gave him a hug around his neck.

"Hi, Dad." My stomach fluttered.

"Hi," he said. He didn't look at me.

"Great to be home," I said under my breath and walked inside.

I got Bridey a drink and rubbed my temples. I could see Mom and Dad talking, or, she was talking. He had his head buried under the truck's hood. A tingly rush of fear washed over me.

The kitchen door opened and Dad stuck his head in.

"Come out here a minute," he grumbled, and lit a cigarette. "Let's walk."

"I'm think I'm too tired, Dad." I didn't want to go on a walk with him.

"C'mon." He started off down the hill and I followed. We got to the edge of the creek and crossed by jumping from flat rock to flat rock. The air was chilly by the water. I wanted him to say something. It was killing me not knowing if he was going to yell at me, or what.

We walked for about fifteen minutes until we came to a waterfall. I had come here many times. I pulled my sweater close around me. Dad lit another cigarette.

"I don't like what happened to your sister," he said. He had to raise his voice so I could hear him over the roar of the water.

"Me neither, Dad." I shoved my hands in my pockets. It had crossed my mind more than once on our little walk that his plan was to toss me in the water.

"Your mother tried to explain some of this to me. She said it's like booze. I think I'd understand it more if you'd gotten into drinking," he said, stubbing his cigarette out in some spongy damp moss.

"Drinking would have made me fat," I said.

"I think if you're worried about getting fat you should not eat so much and exercise more." He looked at me.

"Dad, It's not like that. It's like I turn into someone else, a robot, and I can't stop eating. Then I have to throw it all up so I don't get fat. I can't explain it very well." I felt like I was going to cry again. It was hard for me to talk about it, but I wanted him to understand. "Mom's right. The counselor said it's like alcoholism."

"I'm not very good at this." He was staring at the water again.

"The counselor at the hospital said sometimes it's good for the whole family to go into therapy. That would help you understand. Don't you think that would make you feel better?" I started getting a little excited.

"I'm not going to therapy. I wouldn't be of any help there." He started walking downstream. "C'mon."

"But Dad. I don't just mean for you to talk to some-one to help me, I mean for you. If you don't under-stand, aren't you just going to keep feeling weird around me?" I was feeling less excited. "I don't want you to think I'm gross!"

"Perk, I don't trust therapists and counselors. I don't need some jerk with a diploma to tell me what a bad job I've done as a father. I'd rather have you guys go and fill me in. Then, I'll go to the moon and back to help you."

I didn't think much of his promise to go to the moon for me when he couldn't fathom the journey to a support group.

"Mom has a diploma," I said.

"That's not what I mean. I want to help you. That's

all I wanted to say." He took my hand and ran his rough fingers across my palm. I got a sudden feeling of loss, like he had just died. It made me feel horrible and empty. I threw my arms around him.

He hugged me too and we stood there by the water. I understood why he brought me to the falls. It seemed Dad could only really say what was in his heart when he was near some force of nature. Sometimes I felt we were the same that way. Otherwise he was angry, bottled up, dangerous. What he had actually said to me didn't help, but knowing he wanted to help, did.

"Do you wish I was someone else?" I asked him.

He squeezed me harder. "No. No, not at all. Sometimes I wish I was, though. I wouldn't trade you or your mother or sister in for anyone. It never crossed my mind. I might trade your dog in, though."

"Dad!" I pushed him gently. He pointed and I saw Larry loping across at a shallow part. Mom must have let him out to come get us. We waited for him to catch up and shake water all over. The sun was ready to start sinking behind the hills.

I followed Dad home. I told him about Ms. Bacharach's baby, and I started to tell him about the people I had met in group, but I ran out of steam. I was more tired than I could remember in a long time.

Mom was reading mail in the kitchen when we got home. Bridey was pulling raisins out of a bagel in her high chair.

"So?" Mom looked at us.

"So, we lived." Dad kicked his boots off.

I shrugged and looked at Mom. She put down the mail and came over to me.

"Do you know that we want to help, Perk?" She put her arm around me. Dad got a beer out of the fridge.

"Yeah, Mom." I think I did. It seemed like the best we could all do then. I understood that.

"Dad could drive me to the support groups at the hospital until I get set up with one here in town. That would help me," I said quietly. "You wouldn't have to come in, Dad."

"Let me know when." He finished the last of his beer. "I'm going to take a shower."

"Mom, I want to have some soup, and go to bed." Really, I just wanted to go to bed, but I hadn't eaten anything since the hospital. The counselor said that a good way to keep myself from having another bulimic episode was to remember H.A.L.T. It meant I shouldn't let myself get too hungry, angry, lonely, or tired.

Mom started some soup. "Your dad doesn't want to go to therapy, because he's afraid they'll blame your sickness on him."

I hadn't thought of that. I thought he was worried they would tell him he drank too much. He always seemed to act so tough around me, too tough. So what if he was scared? So was I.

"Maybe you can accept that he's doing the best that he can. We both are."

I went upstairs after dinner. I thought about seeing Evvie and Dom at school tomorrow and a shiver ran through me. I didn't know if I was ready for that. The counselor told me I needed to find someone at school I could talk to and be honest with when things felt overwhelming.

It was all almost too much. But, everything in my life had almost been too much up until now. At least good things were starting to happen now that I had decided to get well.

I threw my jeans on the floor and looked in the mirror. My butt still looked too big. I sighed and climbed into bed. Someday I wouldn't worry about that anymore. Right now I just didn't want it to rule my life.

Larry climbed into bed and flopped across my legs with a groan.

"Get off me, Mutley," I pushed him off.

It was good and bad to be home. After all, everything had started here. I thought about what the counselor said today in group, that these kinds of sicknesses and addictions were a way to not look at what we knew. It scared me to think of what was ahead. I knew I was being brave, though, and that was better than being sick.

That was the last thing I remember thinking before I fell asleep.

Epilogue

❖❖❖❖❖❖❖❖❖

The muscles in my legs burned and my nose was running. The sun glared off of the crunchy surface of the snow like blue and yellow diamonds. I stopped skiing for a minute to catch my breath. The wind blew clean and cold through the valley and I knew my cheeks were bright pink. It felt great. This was my very favorite kind of day. And, it was Christmas morning.

Larry barked at a rabbit standing on the other side of the creek. The rabbit twitched his nose and started a stare contest with Larry.

Mom and I had learned to cross country ski this winter. She never used her skis but I tried to go several times a week. It made me feel strong and clear, like when I was painting. The therapist I've been seeing said it was a good way to get some "quiet time" in my head. She was big on that. She said I'd spent enough time torturing myself, and it would be nice for me to spend some time doing things that made me feel good.

Whatever. But she was right. Things were working for me now and I didn't want to mess them up, so I did what she told me to do.

"Perk! Perk!" I heard Dad yell for me through the woods. The rabbit took off and Larry whined in frustration.

I guessed everyone was up and showered and ready to open presents. I smiled. I loved Christmas.

"Co-ming," I hollered. I pulled my scarf back over my face and set off towards the house.

It was almost a year since I'd been at the hospital. Everything in my life had changed. I had thrown up a couple of times, which made me feel really bad. My therapist said to try and use what I've learned and move on. I try, but sometimes it gets really hard.

I've had to confront Dad about things that hurt my feelings and make me feel bad about myself. Those are the times I feel like I want to eat, a lot. Instead I make phone calls to my friends that I'm in group with. It seems to help.

I started my own recovery group. We meet after school, three days a week. Kids have shown up that I never knew were sick, but then I guess most people didn't know I was sick either.

I have a new best friend, Zan Sturgeon. She's bulimic and started coming to my group on the first day. We got to be good friends right away. I don't really spend time with Evvie anymore, but that's okay. Dom moved to Kingston and the last I heard he had gotten caught stealing another car.

I tried to keep in touch with Jason, but it was hard because we went to different schools. I have a pretty steady boyfriend now, his name is J.P. He's really nice and he likes me a lot. He's also an excellent kisser.

I saw my house through the trees. The Christmas lights twinkled in the window. I saw Mom walking around in the kitchen.

She stuck her head out the door. "Hurry up, Perk. We have some surprise guests!" She rubbed her arms like she was cold and hopped up and down.

I popped my skis off and ran up the hill with them tucked under my arm. I stamped off the snow before I went into the house. Ms. Bacharach and her husband were there with John Henry.

"Merry Christmas, Perk!" She grinned at me.

"Hey! I thought today was my day off," I laughed. I worked in her studio on weekends, and I helped take care of John Henry.

"We brought over your present. I was too excited to wait." She clapped her hands together.

"Wow! What is it? Can I see?"

Ms. Bacharach grabbed my shoulders and steered me into the living room. There was a wooden easel that stood taller than me. It had a huge red bow on it. I recognized it as one that had belonged to her father. He was dead now, but had been a famous local artist.

"Oh my gosh! You can't give this to me!" I was awestruck. It was a completely fantastic present, and I knew it meant a lot to her.

"Of course I can. You deserve it. I've watched you work so hard to get well. You're an inspiration, dear girl." She took my hand. "I'm proud and grateful to have you in my life."

My eyes welled up. I hugged her.

"We're all proud of her," Dad said. He was leaning against the fireplace. When I looked at him he was giving me a little smile that said I was his daughter, and we had a special connection. I hadn't seen that from him too often. It wasn't that I hadn't deserved it before, I just think we had been so far apart from each other for so long there was no place for it.

"All right," Ms. Bacharach announced. "We're off to spread more good cheer." She swept John Henry up to her hip. "I love you, Perk."

"I love you, too. Thanks." I hugged her.

Mr. Bacharach squeezed my arm and smiled.

Bridey stomped in, pulling Larry by his collar. She had a big frown on her face. "I thought we were going to open presents," she said.

"Okay, let's go," Mom said.

I sat on the couch and looked at the tree. I let my eyes get blurry and the tinsel and lights melted into each other. At this moment I felt truly content, and full, and sure of who I was. These moments were one of the best things about getting better, these moments of peace in my head. And I got them more and more often. No more voices. No more demon girl dreams.

Bridey lugged over a present to me and put it on my lap. "Oooh, a big one! Isn't this exciting?"

I gave her an enormous hug. "Yes, my honeybun. It certainly is."

And it was.

...mia
❖❖❖❖

...is a dangerous eating disorder ...recognized and treated properly. Bulimia and its sister illness, anorexia nervosa (self-starvation), claim thousands of new victims each year—primarily adolescents and young women. However, eating disorders can begin later in life and effect some men, as well.

Bulimia is characterized by repeated overeating binges typically followed by forced vomiting. In some cases, people also purge by prolonged fasting, excessive exercise, or abuse of laxatives, enemas, or diuretics.

Eating disorders are accompanied by serious physical and emotional problems. Physical side-effects can include: rotten teeth, digestive disorders, internal bleeding, amenorrhea, malnutrition, anemia, infected glands, and death from cardiac arrest, kidney failure, heart arrhythmia due to electrolyte imbalance, or severe dehydration. Emotional problems can include: low self-esteem, shame, guilt, anger, lying, lack of intimacy and generalized fears.

Between 2-18% of all women develop bulimia, though fewer become anorexic. As with other addictions, eating disorders are often devastating to the families and friends of sufferers.

For some, a successful recovery can be achieved through support from friends and loved-ones; but, treatment is often necessary from health care professionals such as school counselors, psychotherapists, psychiatrists, or dieticians.

Bulimia is a widely misunderstood and rapidly spreading problem. Since the majority of individuals develop eating disorders before their mid-20's, our schools need to offer classes and resources on prevention and intervention.

More information is available by contacting the resources listed on the following pages.

Resources
❖❖❖❖❖❖❖❖❖❖❖

ANAD
National Association of Anorexia Nervosa and
Associated Disorders
Box 7; Highland Park, IL 60035
(708)831-3438
http://www.healthtouch.com/level1/leaflets/anad/anad001.htm
Distributes listing of therapists, hospitals and informative
materials; sponsors support groups, conference, research, and
a crisis hotline.

EDAP
Eating Disorders Awareness and Prevention
603 Stewart St. #803; Seattle, WA 98101
(206)382-3587
http://members.aol.com/edapinc/home.html
Sponsors Eating Disorders Awareness Week annually in Feb-
ruary with a network of state coordinators and programs;
distributes educational information.

Gürze Books
PO Box 2238; Carlsbad, CA 92018
(760)434-7533
http://www.gurze.com
Distributes and publishes books and newsletters; offers free
eating disorders catalogue.

NEDO — National Eating Disorders Organization
6655 S. Yale Ave.; Tulsa, OK 74136
(918)481-4044
http://www.laureate.com/nedo-con.html
Focuses on prevention, education, research, and treatment
referrals; distributes information

To Order

❖❖❖❖❖❖❖❖❖

Copies of **PERK!** *The Story of a Teenager with Bulimia* are available at bookstores and libraries or directly from Gürze Books.

FREE Catalogue

The *Gürze Eating Disorders Bookshelf Catalogue* has more than 100 books and tapes on eating disorders and related topics, including body image, size-acceptance, self-esteem, feminist issues, and more. It is a valuable resource that is handed out by therapists, educators, and other health care professionals throughout the world.

Gürze Books (PRK)
PO Box 2238
Carlsbad, CA 92018
(760) 434-7533
gzcatl@aol.com • www.gurze.com